The

RECKONING

A Slave Shipwreck Saga

Michael Smorenburg

1 3 5 7 9 8 6 4 2

www.MichaelSmorenburg.com/Reckoning
FaceBook.com/MichaelSmorenburg
MichaelStheWriter@gmail.com

House of Qunard Publishing

ISBN Hardback—978-0-6399153-1-9
ISBN Paperbacks—978-0-6399153-2-6
ISBN eBook—978-0-6399153-0-2
ISBN Audio book—978-0-6399153-3-3

Book Front Cover Photo Credit, Copyright ©: Neil Phillips, 2017

DEDICATION

For Francois.
The man who found the original shipwreck.

That wreck turned out to be São José Paquete de Africa,
foundered on the rocks at Clifton in Cape Town, 1794.

It did not have the gold aboard that we sought but it had a
story and legacy infinitely more valuable.

The Reckoning

KARMA.

We all accept that the human brain is more complex by far than an ordinary computer of the 1980s. Yet the lowliest computer of 1980 could, in one millisecond, extract from the few simple lines we call a barcode, a vast library of information—price, producer, batch, etc.

How much more can a brain read from the mask we wear, from our gait, and from a tone of voice?

These things—our expression, the furrows of our face, our bearing and more, are written into us over decades. The scribes of these things are our experiences and thoughts—and these thoughts are in turn read by others who reinforce everything that we become.

Today, at least where constitutions bridle the behavior of those with power, we enjoy some measure of individuality and are mostly treated on merit. But, the history of our species was a place— and in some quarters, these circumstances remain— where individual rights was a meaningless term. We were born into circumstance and expected to bear whatever was dished out to us as the lot that one or another God had directed for us. We simply lived out a script written for us within the strictures and strata of hierarchy.

We were said to have *karma*—good or bad *luck* resulting from our actions (in this or an earlier life).

But is it luck?

Some, in this book, chose a path that let them walk with dignity in spite of circumstance. In the fullness of time they wrote those internal efforts into their outward appearance and reaped the rewards.

Also by Michael Smorenburg:

- The Praying Nun—*Qunard Publishing—2017*

- The Manhattan Event—*Qunard Publishing—2018*

- Ragnarok—*Qunard Publishing—2017*

- LifeGames—*Qunard Publishing—1995 & 2016*

- A Trojan Affair—*Qunard Publishing—2016*

- The Everything Sailing Book Part 2—*Adams Media 1999*

- The Everything Sailing Book Part 1—*Adams Media 1998*

- Business Buyer's Kit—*Career Press 1997*

ACKNOWLEDGMENTS

This is a fictional account that was inspired by a true story.

A tragedy.

In 1794 a slave ship, *São José—Paquete de Africa*, was wrecked along the coast near Cape Town in South Africa. Four hundred slaves were in her holds.

Half that number perished that day.

The survivors were rounded up and marched into town where they were sold to recover costs.

Let us first pause here a moment to remember all four-hundred nameless lives wasted.

That story is already told in the prequel to this novella, *"The Praying Nun—A Slave Shipwreck Saga"*.

To their masters, these slaves were not humans. They were chattel—mere assets.

As such, nobody cared to record their whereabouts or their individual stories. The best we can do is to infer from the general records how their lives may have unfolded.

This story gives a name and ordeal to one of them.

The period in which this story is set was a tumultuous and confusing epoch in the colonies. The French Revolution had created global turmoil and the Dutch East India Company, afraid of seeing the friendly port at the Cape of Good Hope fall into the French enemy hands, requested English help.

An English fleet came ashore and after a brief skirmish with the local Dutch authorities, unaware that the invading force had been directed by their masters in Holland, the English took over the administration in the colony. This invasion was never intended to be permanent. Roman Dutch law and its existing administrators proceeded as before, but under the scrutiny of the British overlords, without those new rulers actively applying English law.

In order to tame this story and avoid its narrative and appeal becoming unnecessarily bogged down by this tangle of confusion, I have taken the liberty of shifting the domestic facts and actual timelines. I have introduced real life figures drawn from history and imported them into these pages. Where it was necessary to make adjustments to actual historical timelines and prominent persons featured, I have aimed to retain the prevailing mood and mores of the time that they presented.

———————

Thank you to darling Kirstin Engelbrecht for your tireless line-by-line edits and putting up with me in all ways.

A massive thank you to my brilliant editor, Karolyn Herrera for a sterling job.

For this cover, matched as it is to my other three titles, I give special thanks to Southern Stiles Designs and Gemma Poppet for her creativity and astounding work ethic. And I thank Neil Phillips for the use of the cover photo, necessarily edited as it had to be.

Thanks to all proof-readers and especially my good friend, Carel Hauptfleisch who always motivates me just when I think it's a waste of time.

Thanks to all who have given me so much encouragement to keep writing.

Chapter 1

Cape of Good Hope, tip of Africa
June/Winter, 1794

Brittle as fine china, mussel shells baked colourless by countless African noons clinked and shattered under the heel of a boot.

The sound of it yanked Chikunda to his feet.

A rough club in his hand, he crouched like a knife-fighter covering his pregnant wife, terror coursing through his veins.

"There'll be no need for that," the man with an unruly mop of coal black hair and glinting blue eyes rumbled in a coarse Portuguese dialect, the yawning mouth of his battered old blunderbuss aimed at Chikunda's chest and a fawn-coloured mongrel, tall as his knee, at his heel.

The young pye-dog had a friendly demeanour and well-kept coat. One ear stood urgently to attention, the other only at half-mast, its attention keenly tuned to its master.

The weapon in the stranger's hands was swaying. The man was dangerously nervous, his ragged breathing betraying fear, or perhaps worse, excitement.

"Put it down," he ordered Chikunda.

He was a small man, slight of build with hands as gnarled as the granite boulders strewn all around Chikunda's makeshift encampment on the shell-littered beach.

"You are the shipwreck survivors?" he accused, "from the slaver?"

"Who are you? How do you know I speak Portuguese?" Chikunda challenged.

"You're in no position to negotiate, my friend," the man said. A smile of respect started to grin through. "I've been watching you since you came ashore."

"Two moons?"

"Two moons," the man agreed. "Two months you've been here. Did you think you could stay like this forever? Here in my little paradise?" He paused. "Put that thing down and tell me your names."

The gun was still swaying.

Chikunda's woman had steadily crept around behind him, taking cover behind his legs.

Since the sinking of their ship, the runaway slaves Chikunda and Mkiwa—or *Faith*, as she preferred to be called—had been holed up on this small rocky peninsula, subsisting on the bounties of the sea and drinking from the burbling brook of sweet clean water that this lucky place had provided.

"I am Chikunda… my wife, Faith."

Gently, Chikunda set his club down beside Faith, knowing that she would have it back into his hand the instant he called for it—*Pitisha*! Pass it!—in their Swahili tongue.

"Please don't make me use this. Throw it further away, Faith," the man ordered. "I'm not taking chances with a desperate man."

"What is it you want?" Chikunda challenged, as his wife did the man's bidding, kicking the club out of reach as if it was a serpent.

"Good. Thank you." The blue eyes relaxed a little, taking the ancient shotgun away from his shoulder but still training it on Chikunda from four paces away. "What do I want?" the man repeated. "I'd think it would be obvious."

"Is there a reward?" Chikunda asked simply.

This was a white man, a Portuguese white man. The slave ship that had marooned the couple here had been a Portuguese vessel; the port of Cape Town was only just over that nearby ridge.

Things weren't looking good.

Lucky to survive the stormy tempest and under the cloak of darkness, the pair of fugitives had slipped away from the carnage of the shipwreck and found this secluded refuge. Well as it had treated them, it was a place hemmed in by geography, trapping them with steep cliffs to the north and a military garrison encamped near a beach to the south, with towering mountains to the east and a wild ocean to the west.

When they'd come ashore, weeks of starvation, previous ill treatment, and vicious beatings had left them near death's door.

Only by Chikunda's determination, God's grace, and their prayers, had they survived and found this enclave of peace. They'd agreed that they'd need a month, perhaps two, to recover themselves sufficiently for the long trek that lay ahead if they were ever to reach home again.

Now, right at the threshold of that deadline, this stranger had stumbled into the hidden camp.

Mozambique was an unknown walking distance to the north. Sailing south in the stinking slave ship had taken 24 days, but there was no way to convert this to a return journey on foot. All they agreed upon was that they must try, but it would be a monumental task and they needed to be healthy first.

It had been a race against time.

The man had caught them unawares, relaxing in the late afternoon sun, somewhere between the high alert of the terrifying first days and the creeping complacency of a routine.

The only other humans they'd seen were redcoats encamped in garrison across the water of the bay to their south.

They'd also seen this shaggy-haired man foraging close by, but he had somehow never seemed to notice them.

He appeared to be a man of habit and his frequent visits, except for today, had been quite predictable.

It had been one moon since Faith had missed her monthly bleed when they'd been loaded aboard the wicked vessel, and it had been two more moons since then until now.

She was now starting to show and the trip to escape would become increasingly perilous with each passing day of her pregnancy.

Calculating the moment to make their break for it had plagued Chikunda... and now, it seemed, they had just run out of luck.

"You've been watching me," the man said, ignoring the question of reward. "And I've also been watching you." He began to smile. "But you never knew it."

There was no ridicule in the smile, no cruelty. Quite the contrary; the man's eyes seemed to moisten with emotion and the peculiar gentleness of someone who knows by experience the suffering of others.

This meant one of two things—he was a friend or he was stark crazy.

"Why wait two months?" Chikunda challenged. Fate had them in its icy grip; only courage under fire might let them go where it would lead and do so with dignity.

"I had no need of it until now," the man answered plainly, putting the scattergun down and holding his palms open to the couple to emphasize that he meant no threat. "You have not been at risk until now."

"Been at risk?"

"Do you think I'm the only one who knows that where there is repeatedly smoke there must be a regular fire maker?"

Chikunda instantly understood.

"I have kept the fire small and only in the twilight in our cave facing the sea?" Chikunda defended with the intonation of a question, more in apology to Faith who had argued that they should make no fire at all.

The man laughed, his eyes twinkling again and his dog seemed to relax with it too, and moved from his side, inspecting the site with its nose.

"This is a dry land, prone to wild fires. So, everyone is always alert to the smell of smoke. The wind sometimes blows this way, or that…" He indicated the two bays on either side of the headland they were on. "And the fire watch at the garrison must be constantly vigilant for smoke on the wind." He shrugged sadly.

"You are here to arrest us?" Chikunda felt the need to bring the conversation to its head. To know their fate.

"Arrest you? Me? On my own? Without shackles?" He asked it rhetorically and then squinted to answer. "Mind you, I would not have to share the reward then, and with that thing," he said, indicating his rusting, ugly, old weapon lying in the grass, "you'll go wherever I point you, no? And she'll go where you go."

"If not arrest, then what?"

The agony of having their fate drawn out like this was crippling.

Faith has suffered enough, he thought. This was the moment he must make up his mind for fight or flight... or surrender.

"A warning, my friend. I am sorry I have made you uncomfortable. This is not sport for me, but I needed to know your temperament. A caged man is a dangerous one, and I have a simple but pleasant life that I don't wish to complicate."

"I'm not understanding," Chikunda offered. "Why warn us?"

"Because I too am a fugitive. You are a fugitive," he shrugged. "We at least have that in common, eh?"

"How does a fugitive know so much about the reward for another man?"

"Because this is a British colony and I am a fugitive not from these masters, but from my own people, from the Portuguese. You are a fugitive from the Portuguese too."

Chikunda stood, dumbstruck, gaping at the man, suddenly feeling exhausted in the wake of certain doom having passed.

"I think it unwise to waste time in more idle chatter," suggested the man, picking up his weapon once more with his left hand and offering his right hand in friendship. "I live yonder, across there."

He pointed in the direction of the smaller bay to the north of this headland, to a crease in the mountain slope directly above where the slave ship had wrecked and below a vast granite outcrop high on the mountain.

"The Dutch were the masters here when I deserted my ship. They call the bay after me, Schoenmakers Gat, Cobblers Cave. I'm the shoemaker, Sebastião de Malagrida, most pleased to make your acquaintance." He indicated the mutt and motioned with his head for it to follow, "Jack."

The dog's ears went up and he trotted over with enthusiasm, whipping his tail furiously. Chikunda patted him.

The two men broke off the prolonged handshake of comrades. "I can give you shelter… not for long, but for longer than you can safely stay here," he promised. "Collect your stuff."

A short time later they were picking their way through the hardy scrub with its gnarled woody roots set into beach sand between the granite boulders.

They came up onto the ridge of land that was the southern boundary to the shoemaker's bay.

There they paused a moment on the vast granite rock outcrop that stood taller than a ship's mast at the southern headland of the bay. It formed the natural breakwater that had given shelter to the stricken slave ship as it limped in and wrecked on a rocky reef in the middle of that bay.

"I watched the unfolding tale of your wreck," Sebastião pointed, "from my vantage place up there."

He indicated again the small valley that ran down from the brooding mountain backdrop to the bay.

"Why did you not come to our assistance?" Chikunda demanded, offering his hand to his wife to help her over a fracture between the rocks.

"I could see it was a Portuguese ship," Sebastião reminded him. "Their gratitude for my assistance would not surpass their lust to see my desertion punished," he predicted. "I have a good enough life here and I'm not about to risk it. Almost not for anything."

"Yet you help us?"

"A fair question," he responded. "If God has seen fit to save you from the tempest and deliver you from your owners, and God has seen fit to allow you this time to recover, then it is a small risk for me to win a little favor by lending my efforts to see you on your way."

"On our way?"

"You don't look like anybody from these parts. You're never going to fit in. You're going to have to move north or east. Anywhere but here."

"You say you have been watching us?"

"Aye."

"For how long?"

He laughed.

"I told you. From your first day you settled in."

"You do know that we have been watching you also."

"Sure. No harm in that. I saw you watching me many times when I came to harvest my sustenance. I thought it prudent to not let on that I'd seen you notice me. My little game. It is small entertainment in an otherwise unceasing procession of mildly pleasant days." He turned back and looked out over the tumble of rocks and the pools they formed, choked as they were with kelp and life. "This is the best place to collect seafood in most any weather." He laughed again at something that moved behind his eyes, "You've been living in my pantry."

Throughout their stay, Chikunda and Faith had watched this man coming regularly to collect shellfish.

They'd imagined that their hide was well enough camouflaged and that they'd avoided his detection.

It was unsettling to know that they had been duped.

The man seemed to have a routine. Every third day he would arrive at low tide and leave with a bounty of lobster and other snail-like sea life, penguin and seabird eggs and even kelp.

They'd then seen the wisps of his fire rising from that valley they were now picking their way toward through the hardy waist-high bush.

"You say that they have detected us?"
"Sure."

"How do you know this?"

"You have a short memory or don't think very broadly," he said in a joking tone. "I'm the shoemaker, I mend the boots for the soldiers in the next bay, Baai van von Kamptz. They're preparing to extract you back to the town."

"When?"

"Probably any time now, they only just learned about you. The grog, you see. Out of the way, most of the time this lot are smashed out of their minds on an evil brew. I thought it best not to seem too interested when they told me."

"A big risk then?"

"There's no reason for them to think I'd harbor you, is there?"

"You're a good man then?"

"Perhaps." He shrugged. "Or stupid, or one in need of a heavenly reward."

"Do they know who we are?"

"Who else could you be? The other two hundred of your fellows were sold in the town the day after the wreck," he confirmed. "Perhaps half still in the colony now; the rest shipped to other shores or trekked inland with their new masters."

It was the first confirmation that Chikunda had about his fellow slaves who had survived the wreck.

If two hundred had been saved, then it was another two hundred that had drowned on that dreadful day two months ago when he'd made his escape.

From their current elevation as they made their way to the shoemaker's home, Chikunda looked across the bay and down onto the wreck site. The beach was now entirely clear of corpses, eaten by gulls, tides and other scavengers.

Some of the wreckage was still strewn about up near the highest tidemark, and only one or two beams still jutted above the waterline marking the spot, trapped between the tumble of rocks just behind the crashing waves.

Arriving at the hill's brow, where the steep slope paused before soaring into the clouds, they picked their way northward through the bush along a rough foot track.

Nearing the end of that contoured path around the bay, at what looked from a distance like a dead end to the pathway, they came to a rock hovel inside of a cave with a lean-to of planking and canvas at its entrance.

"It's not much," the shoemaker admitted, "but it keeps me dry."

"Me" was about all there was room for.

"Don't fret." The Portuguese saw the concern written across his new friends' faces. "It has an atrium… the cave proper."

Chikunda and Faith had no possessions to speak of, so they added little to the clutter.

Down at the beach, they had managed to salvage rags from three of the dead crew that had washed ashore in the days after the wreck. From the naked slaves that had littered the beach, they could salvage nothing at all.

'Atrium' had been a grandiose exaggeration.

At the back of the cave was a false termination.

Sebastião dragged his rickety wardrobe made from flotsam aside to reveal a fissure in the rock. In the flickering candlelight, it looked like the granite itself had fractured and part of it had fallen away.

They squeezed into the void and there beyond its mouth was space enough for all of them to stand upright. There was enough room to lie down as well.

It was cool and dank and a little claustrophobic, with only the sound of water dripping somewhere in the deep recesses of darkness beyond the reach of the small dancing candle flame.

The floor was packed earth and the cobbler seemed to use this hiding place as his store for a clutter of tatty valuables evidently salvaged from the shore.

"You can stay here some days," he offered. "Not indefinitely, but long enough to learn from me about what you face, and long enough for the people who seek you to lose interest."

"Can you guess at how long?"

"Not much longer than a week, two at the maximum, I'm afraid."

"Faith is pregnant. We dare not wait even that long."

"You'd be advised to not make it much less than that either. The heat needs to be off and you have much to learn about this land, where to navigate and where not to venture. You're in a bit of a bind."

Chapter 2

Morning came in the pitch black of the dungeon, the jailer's voice speaking English beyond the shaft of light cutting through the pitch.

It was a moment of terror for Chikunda.

In the dank and musty prison, his mind whirled to make sense of it. How he had landed here, captured.

Three men's voices were audible, but only their tone, not their words.

Though he stumbled to speak it, Chikunda could understand English well enough if he could also read the talker's lips, but not at all when it was obscured by thick walls.

Through that cartwheeling terror, the memory came back to him—they were still in the Portuguese shoemaker's cave.

Faith's breathing still whispered softly in sleep. In the cold, she had burrowed in under him and he gently traced her body to understand how she lay. The warmth of her head like a kitten, the soft purr of her breathing even paced and relaxed.

Satisfied that he could extract himself without disturbing her, he groped to his left. The earthen ground was there and so was the damp rock wall.

He rose to a crouch and tucked the filthy blanket back in around Faith to let her sleep on.

The jail wasn't to keep him in. Right now, it was to keep them out—whoever they were.

He gingerly approached the slit of light coming in past the makeshift cupboard that was the door to his hidden cave. Listening actively, almost feeling his ears twisting and turning like that of a cat, he examined the sounds for any hint of attitude in the voices.

They sounded dire.

The cobbler was doing much of the babble, answering curt questions that were fired at him, making light of the conversation. Chikunda couldn't discern what was being asked, but they had the intonation of questions.

Very slowly the jovial Portuguese ex-sailor won the men over and gruff laughter was heard.

The voices moved out of the cave.

Presently, the sound of horse hooves danced the little signature jig of animals being mounted and having their heads turned to depart.

They went away at a trot.

Chikunda waited in the darkness and then Faith started to stir, her hushed voice confused and in Swahili.

"Sh—sh—sh—my dove. There are men outside," he whispered urgently.

He explained to her what he had discerned—
that men on horses, at least two of them, had
interrogated their host.

Sebastião came humming back into his hovel,
exaggerating the sounds of tidying up and busying
himself in the manner of a long-time bachelor.

Unsure of the normal pattern of the man's
routines, Chikunda and Faith remained silent in
the dark, erring on the side of caution. Mindful
that one of the inquisitors may still be about or
double back, he presumed that Sebastião was
deliberately retaining cover for this possibility.

Eventually, after what seemed like eternity
hearing the muted sounds from outside and the
repetitive drip—drip—drip in the cold blackness,
Chikunda decided that the time must come to
break cover.

He manufactured a light cough.

"Ahhh," he heard from beyond the cupboard
and Jack barked his own reminder that he knew
they were there.

A moment later, it creaked aside, wobbly on
poorly made legs. Light and Jack burst
exuberantly into their world.

"They are alive!" The blue eyes twinkled. "My
friends, we had visitors. They were most anxious
to meet you."

"You told them we are here?!"

"Of course not. I would now be in irons and
you would be in worse. Come, Jack... out," he
laughed and the dog bolted out of the cave,
expecting a game. "It was the Sergeant at Arms
and his aide, galloped up from the von Kamptz

garrison two miles yonder. My prediction came true, they raided your camp last night and were in an evil mood at your escape."

"What did you tell them?"

"Only that I haven't seen you. It made them more than a little suspicious because they know that's where I collect my dinner. I had to admit that I had seen you before. I told them I only saw you from a distance and thought you were simply *Hottentots... Hotnots*, snuck back to your traditional home."

"I don't understand," Chikunda frowned.

"Forgive... this piece of coast used to be wandered by the Khoikhoi people, the *Hotnots*. The Dutch call them Hottentots. There were also the evil little Bushmen here with their poisoned arrow tips. They were all chased out when the German, von Kamptz, built his homestead there, in the *'Baai van von Kamptz'*. The Hotnots are a treacherous lot. We must perpetually keep our eye out for them. They'll steal anything not nailed down. The garrison moves them out if they find them."

"Did they believe you?"

"Not until I gave them grog and invited them back for more."

"They're coming back?"

"Perhaps."

"When?"

"Hard to tell. But not today. Not for some days, I would imagine. It is rare that anyone passes this way. I go weeks without seeing a soul. This morning the old man looked rough.

Probably drank his anger away when you had slipped through his fingers. Need breakfast? I have biscuits left." He fished behind a tatty curtain on a rickety shelf. "Bit old, stale and moldy but edible. The last of the lobster we eat later."

He offered them little brown blobs, each wearing a forest of translucent fur.

"We don't want to use your scarce resources," Chikunda answered for the look Faith wore across her face.

"Suit yourself," the cobbler replied without judgment and put the tin aside, taking his ancient blunderbuss down from its hook above the doorway and checking its mechanism.

His action prompted Chikunda to clear up what seemed obvious.

"I am concerned. We are putting you in grave danger."

"Some," Sebastião admitted. "It depends on the circumstances. If they'd ransacked and found you hidden at the back," he paused with a shrug of his shoulders and mouth, "I'd be in chains and dragged to the dungeon at the old fort in Cape Town. Something, you can imagine, I don't relish. But I'll be honest with you now. If I get caught with you in my presence, to save myself I must claim I have you under arrest. You understand? I am *friendly* to you, I'm not yet your friend."

"I understand," Chikunda agreed. "If it came to it, we are duty bound to do our all to repay your kindness by not contradicting that."

"I don't mean to be rude," Sebastião asked now of Faith, "but do you not talk at all? Do you not understand the tongue?"

She answered to the floor, whispering something in a tiny voice.

"She fears men," Chikunda spoke for her. "She means no rudeness by it, but beyond the priests at her convent, her experience with white men and Arabs has not been the best."

"Understandable," Sebastião agreed. "I'm sorry. I meant no offense asking so directly."

"It was fair to ask."

"It is time I cut wood." Perhaps to ease the discomfort of the moment, Sebastião picked up an axe and made his way toward a grove, Jack at his heel.

Within minutes, Chikunda had joined him, drawn by the thud of the axe.

"Let me take a spell," the broad-shouldered black man offered, putting out his hand to take the axe.

"I won't say no." Sebastião mopped his brow and stood back to watch.

The axe arched high and fell on the log, splintering it with a single blow.

"Perhaps a little less vigor," the Portuguese suggested, admiration in his voice.

"This is not difficult work," Chikunda insisted.

"Aye... but it's the only axe I have and it may think that your handling of it is out of sorts."

"Understood." Chikunda went to diligent work with less enthusiasm. "How far did you sail?" he asked of the Portuguese, enjoying the company of a man after such a long spell.

"Past this cape," the cobbler pointed south, "and around it and toward the rising sun, many moons. Maybe four moons of sailing to a new land, an island kingdom where the men are small but ferocious. Smaller than me but with slanted pitiless eyes."

"Smaller than you even?" Chikunda's face was a mask of mirth and the Portuguese laughed.

"Hard to believe, no? Yes. But any one of them would chop you down with empty hands faster than you destroy that log."

"This I would like to see," Chikunda said it with the confidence of having been a master at stick fighting and unarmed combat in his village.

"They are fierce, my friend. Taught me tricks—where to land a blow, how to plant my feet and turn my hips. How to divert an attacker's energy and tangle him in his own limbs and choke him with his own garments if it comes to that."

"This you can do? You learnt these ways?"

"I learned what I could from the fishermen of the village where our ship docked."

"You could teach me these things?"

"I can hint at them. I'm no more than a beginner myself, but in this world, one never knows when it might be useful, eh?"

Chikunda kept the head of the axe travelling in thudding circles, out-round-chop-yank.

It was brutally hot work, the blast of a furnace-like wind descending upon them down the mountain out of the northeast.

Round and round the axe head sped, splinters flew and lengths of firewood piled up into an impressive stack. Rivulets of sweat ran freely down Chikunda's torso, his muscles oiled and resembling a fine statue celebrating the best of the human condition.

When he was done, the Portuguese showed him some of what he had learned about self-defense and attack in the far away land of little people.

"These men make war with their hands only?"

"Oh, no," the shoemaker shook his head. "There is a class who carry with them swords. Always two great big swords stuck in their sash, in their belt."

"Swords?" Chikunda was unfamiliar with the term.

"Ahhhh of course. It is not a weapon of your people. Like large knives, as long as your arm."

"I understand. I have seen these but not seen them used. What do they call this place?" Chikunda asked with a tone to his voice that suggested he might want to travel there.

"Nippon. I doubt there has ever been a black man there. You would be quite the spectacle. You learn fast," he remarked.

"My parents taught me that it is more important to be curious than to be obedient."

"I'm not sure that the one is an alternative for the other," Sebastião suggested, "but perhaps it doesn't translate well from your tongue. But it is a good attitude, nonetheless. You say you worked with sticks?"

"It is customary, yes. Young boys fight with reeds, men go on to use sticks... like this one."

Chikunda picked up a discarded length of pole thicker than his thumb and half as tall as he stood. He scratched through the offcuts to find another similar one. Jack bounced on his front legs, expecting a game of fetch.

"We hold them like this," Chikunda instructed, ignoring him.

In his left fist, he grasped near its center. His right fist gripped the attacking stick by its end and then he moved about in fluid steps, fighting an imaginary foe.

The left spun and parried like a shield while his right wrist deftly flicked the attacking pole. In his fist, it was a lethal weapon, droning a mournful hum as it cut through the air in an unceasing whirl of motion.

"Most impressive," Sebastião applauded. "I would like to see you wield a sword. You would be deadly with one in each hand, in the Nippon style. I think that I'll show you my prize possessions, but first we must move this mountain."

They loaded up with cut wood and made their way back to the dwelling, packing the logs out.

They ate the last of the lobster that the Portuguese kept in his larder of sorts.

"They'll keep alive two days if I keep this hemp sacking wet and cold. By the third day, I must collect more," he explained. "The people of Nippon taught me to forage. If it hadn't been for them, I might well have starved, as so many sailors do when wrecked on your wild coast."

Chikunda cocked his head, inviting details.

"Kelp, you have forests of it here. Quite edible when you learn how to prepare it and acquire the taste."

"I saw you collecting it too," Chikunda nodded sagely. "I wondered what you were doing with it. Can you show me?"

"Indeed. You may need it someday, if…"

The cobbler left the matter open ended.

"These mementos you brought," Chikunda referred back to the weapon that the Portuguese had hinted at. "May I see them?"

Sebastião wore an expression of some regret. It said that in a moment of camaraderie, he had shared too much information.

"These are valuable to me," he told Chikunda before moving. "I have never told anyone about them, much less shared the sight of my darlings."

"If you are uncomfortable…" Chikunda didn't finish.

"I'm not comfortable," Sebastião admitted. "But I feel the urge. They are too magnificent to be kept so long without the praise they deserve."

He stood and disappeared behind the cupboard that was temporarily Chikunda and Faith's room.

"What is he fetching?" Faith quizzed. She had been steadily tidying the place.

"He has weapons from a faraway place. Large daggers I believe."

"Do you trust this man?" she asked in Swahili.

"Strangely… with my life. He has already saved ours. We owe him a life and perhaps more than that."

The cobbler reappeared carrying a length of canvass wrapped around something weighty.

He laid it on the rickety homemade bench that doubled as a dining table and workspace, and carefully began to unwrap his prize.

When the stiff fabric was put aside, two weapons lay before them, both with similarly long and intricately patterned handles. With great reverence, the small man picked up the larger of the two weapons and with a whisper, it slid gleaming and glinting out of its scabbard, three feet of flashing brilliance.

"Beware not to test the edge," Sebastião warned. "It will slice you to the bone before you even realize you have touched it."

He handed it over to Chikunda lying flat across the upturned palms of both his hands, but he wore the worried look of a mother cat when she allows her kittens to be handled.

Chikunda felt a breath of whistle fluting through his teeth. The thing seemed to be alive in his hands.

"It is beautiful." The natural warrior in him almost choked at the touch of it.

"And most deadly," Sebastião assured.

Down the entire length of the blade, swam a most handsome undulation of subtle patterns in the steel.

"I have never seen anything quite like it," Chikunda was mesmerized.

"This is the cutting sword. They call it a katana. The other is the companion sword, for stabbing and disemboweling."

Faith kept an eye on the weapons as if serpents had been brought into the little cave, also detecting their lethal proportions.

"When they kill, it is not with brute force," Sebastião explained. "They draw the weapon across the target—slashing and cutting all in one movement. When I saw you move with the sticks and watched the travel of the blows, I had a sense that you would appreciate the magnificence of my trophies."

Carefully, he resheathed and then rewrapped his prizes and disappeared to sequester them away.

"What are you planning?" Faith asked in Swahili in the absence of the Portuguese.

"Nothing, my dove. Just idle men's chatter. Getting to know one another. This man has an unusual grace and refinement for such an outcast."

"We too are now outcasts, and I hold that we keep our grace," she responded.

"I think this is what the man saw in us, and I in him."

Sebastião re-emerged from the antechamber.

"Do you want to see your shipwreck from this high angle?" the shoemaker posed.

"If it's safe enough and the visitors are well away by now, it would be interesting."

They ducked out of the cave mouth and Sebastião led Chikunda another hundred paces, following the gently ascending mountain track winding toward the northern boundary of the bay.

Faith elected to remain behind, keen to clean the place, she told Chikunda.

"Not too much," he cautioned her in Swahili. "We don't know this man's temperament."

"Why did you desert?" Chikunda quizzed the Portuguese man as they ambled, Jack running ahead with that one ear pricked, always alert to threats and opportunities, manufacturing some if none presented themselves.

"Life on the ocean wasn't for me," he answered plainly.

"Why did you go to sea then?"

"I didn't. I didn't choose to. My father had debts and no options."

"How bad can it be?" Chikunda didn't think the crew on the slaver had it too bad—*or was it just relative circumstance that had bent his mind?* he wondered to himself.

"The biscuits you refused for breakfast? That would have been a banquet."

"Why so poor?"

"Crew aren't the owner or the captain's guests or friends. They are tools. Expendable tools."

They reached a granite boulder extending twice their head height on the sea side of the path.

From its perch above the bush they could scan the whole bay, all of its beaches and down onto the ocean flat as a lake and clear as spirits. Rock outcrops divided the beach into four equal parts. Dark fingers of rocky reef and kelp reached from the shore out toward the center of the bay where the water became too deep to discern the white sand from the outcrops.

"What do they do with my people," Chikunda quizzed.

"Beyond the sea? Well, there is another great land out there," he waved toward the western horizon. "The Americas they are called. Two continents… Like your Africa, two large landmasses. I believe that your ship was bound for *Terra de Santa Cruz*… for Brazil. A place where, it is said that farms reach as far as the eye can see. They need your labor."

Chikunda contemplated the possibility of it, of a land beyond sight.

Jack held vigil on the path below the men, whimpering sulkily at being abandoned at path-level.

"Can we see this land? If we climb this mountain behind us perhaps?"

The Portuguese laughed at the thought.

"No, my friend. It is too far. Not days, not weeks, but—like Nippon—months of sailing."

"Months? Moons?"

"Moons, yes. And it is below the horizon. Far below. This earth under our feet is round. You understand? Like a… a…"

Much to Jack's delight, he jumped down from their perch, scouted and picked up a rock of approximate spherical shape then climbed back up.

"Like this. We would be here, you see, and then the other land would be there… and Nippon," he sought a spot almost on the opposite side of the rock to touch his finger to, "would be there."

Sebastião held the spherical rock with three fingers touching its surface approximately all equally distant from one another.

Chikunda eyed him carefully for a hint of humour, as though he might peel into laughter for tricking a gullible victim with such an outlandish claim.

"You are surely joking?"

"No," the cobbler sighed. "It is not my specialty or training. I can tell you no more than that as a fact, to take or to leave."

"Hmmmm," Chikunda frowned, puzzling the possibility. "Are there no people there to do this work?"

"Truly… yes. Yes, I believe there are. But quite why they don't use them, I cannot answer either. I am, at best, a shoemaker and, at worst, a failed sailor. My mind is no better than yours, my little knowledge belongs to others."

They sat in silence a while, the conversation echoing in their heads.

Down below, next to a rock pinnacle that looked like a cherry placed atop the water in the low tide, was the barest outline of the wrecked slave ship.

"Most days, the waves down there where you wrecked are fierce. In winter storms it is a cauldron. Someday, the last of that wreck will all be gone without a trace," Sebastião predicted. "Nobody will know what great drama played out here."

Chikunda nodded in agreement. He'd seen how swiftly the Atlantic had swallowed the evidence of her cruelty.

"Where were we when you saw us?"

"Yonder," Sebastião answered, pointing halfway to the horizon and halfway down the coast to where a big prominent mountain stood in relief, obscuring whatever lay further to the south of it. "It was a vile day and I felt pity for whoever found themselves on this mercilous ocean that afternoon."

He pointed west, to a spot out in the deep, perhaps a nautical mile or more out to sea.

"You can't see it now, but there is a deep and hidden reef there. I watched your ship on its northward tack, tracking directly toward it, my elevation up here giving me the full scope of what was happening and about to happen."

"We saw the waves," Chikunda recalled. "Perhaps as tall as our mast when the squall cleared and the source of that booming thunder was revealed."

"Aye. Your Master must have been an experienced man. I saw him veer from it with no more than three ship lengths of safety. And then you came in here, under this cliff."

His finger traced in agreement with Chikunda's precise memory.

"I saw that reef loom too," Chikunda pointed to the pinnacle just a cable in distance out from the cherry-shaped rock on which they had ultimately foundered."

"I was surprised that your captain did not make for the safe haven of that beach over there, in behind the ridge where I found you yesterday."

"I believe he tried," Chikunda confirmed, "but our steering was broken."

"How does a slave chained in the holds know so much?" The Portuguese eyed him suspiciously. "Come to think of it… how did this slave manage to avoid drowning with his fellows? Or did you escape after being saved?"

"It is complicated," Chikunda was unsure of the dangers or advantages of saying more.

"Now this sounds most intriguing," those blue eyes squinted. "I have time and curiosity. I'm sure you can imagine, after saving you from certain peril… well. I feel I deserve better than secrecy… my home open to you."

Chikunda explained how, when loaded aboard, Alfonso Oliveira, the bosun who was in charge of discipline, a wicked rotund man with a nose like a red bulb, had taken exception to Chikunda's bearing on sight.

How this man had branded him with particular cruelty and relish.

He lifted his shirt to show the Portuguese man the wicked cicatrices of new scar tissue, his left nipple swallowed by the angry keloid welts that looked like coarse and knotted ropes under the skin.

Even accustomed to the ravages that a cruel life could visit on its victims, Sebastião grimaced at the sight of it.

Chikunda described how, when Antonio Pereira, the Captain of the ship *São José de Afrika*, had intervened, an evidently long brewing tension between the men had come to its head.

Upon learning that Chikunda was a devout Christian and that his wife, Faith, was also, the captain—citing the English law that no Christian could be taken into slavery, perhaps to irk the bosun—had spared the couple passage below decks and he had given them privileges that had kept them alive.

When the prospect of the ship's grounding became obvious, the bosun had ordered Faith and Chikunda chained to one another through a hawsehole on the deck.

As the ship had groaned on the slacking tide, hard aground on the reef, fate had intervened and broken her back, freeing the couple from their chained imprisonment in the black of night. Under the cover of that darkness, they had made landfall and escaped to the safe haven six cables in distance south along the coast, to where Sebastião had eventually spied and then confronted them.

"I have heard of this man, of this bosun, Alfonso. He's a butcher." The cobbler nodded gravely and spat as if the mere thought of him brought bile to his mouth. "A crueler bastard, they say, has never darkened these shores."

The whites of Chikunda's eyes became beacons against the anthracite black of his tropical skin.

"He is about? You speak in the present, as if he dwells here still."

"Indeed," Sebastião nodded bleakly. "The captain of your ship and most of that crew have found passage out on other ships. You have chosen tumultuous times to drop in on this little colony." The shoemaker grunted at his own understatement. "Governorship here is far from settled. The Dutch governor still packing, the English Admiral holding the fort, the townsfolk and farmers confused as to who their master may be. Your shipmates—those other wretches like you, salvaged as they were from that storm—were sold the day after you wrecked to defray costs and the money owed to crew paid. It is said that this Alfonso pig lost most of his earnings in the taverns of the towns and on the whores. He is as marooned as you are. Though now, I understand, he has better prospects."

Chikunda had stood on blind impulse and was frantically pacing the small pinnacle that had been their throne for the last several minutes.

Jack gave a yap of elation that his isolation seemed at its end.

Chikunda heard nothing but the terror echoing within his head. The terror of it projected from his eyes, his vision fixed far and distant, as if he was already fleeing toward the horizon.

"Better prospects?" he quizzed, a frown furrowing his brow.

"The drunken old Dutch executioner in the town has lost the stomach for torture. He leaves that to his new assistant, who, I'm told, relishes in it."

There was no need to connect dots any further.

"Does he know about us?" Chikunda's pitch rising sharply, sweat prickling on his brow.

"In all likelihood, by now, yes." Sebastião did not coat it. "I'll wager, he's setting up a posse and bounty hunters. You might be his ticket out of here, you see."

"Ticket?" Chikunda's fingers were knitted behind his head, his elbows almost touching, his forearms trying to crush the anguish out of his brain.

"You're legally still his property. He's the most senior officer of that slave ship left on this coast. If he finds you, you belong to his ship and therefore to him."

"We must go then," Chikunda made to bound down off the rock, his body language signaling that they make haste back to the cave to begin fleeing.

"Sit down," Sebastião insisted. "Running now is the worst thing you can do. Now is the time for a cool and calculating head. I convinced the garrison that you would have escaped along the coast, south toward that mountain. That's where they'll send the search."

"What is in that direction, behind the mountain?" he asked, indicating southward.

"Another bay, Chapman's Bay it is called. It used to be a great wooded valley they say. A bay of *hout*—that's 'wood' in the Dutch tongue— much of it cut down now. Sand dunes and a few fishermen are left. Beyond that, is a tall cliff, Chapman's Peak—it is impassable. There is a pass to the east, between the mountains, up a valley and river. If you cross through there, you are onto flat lands, sand dunes and scrub for two days' walk. And then you reach the mountains again— the rest of Africa—Hottentots Holland they call that mountain range. It is a wild place, but you look like quite a wild man and may survive."

"And my wife?"

"Rough going, especially with another mouth to feed, my friend. You could stick to the coast at the Hottentots Holland. Rumor has it that there is a community of runaway slaves somewhere along that coast. The *drosters*, they're called. Dangerous men living at the boundary of desperation. I'm not sure I'd take a wife and child there." He paused. "Besides, the day will come when their owners in the town and out on the farms will want them back or at least avenge their losses. There will be hell to pay."

"And this path?" Chikunda indicated the extension of the track that they had walked up from the cave dwelling. It snaked its way further to the north and out of sight around a headland.

"It descends back to the coast, but you can't take it." He grimaced. "It leads down and along a narrow coastal plain where cattle graze and directly into the town. The town blocks the entire passage beyond, from Table Bay beach to the lower slopes of Table Mountain. There is no way through in this direction, my friend. The first structure you'll come to on this path will be your old friend Alfonso's place of work at Gallows Hill. It sits between us and the settlement, overlooking the ships at anchor. These people, the Dutch and English, are most macabre in that way. It is the finest view that any scaffold you don't wish to stand on could have... and the bodies regularly dance at the end of a rope there, providing fine and free entertainment for the sailors at anchor too. The only way out for you is along that path to the south to Chapman's Bay," he declared, pointing, "or perhaps up and over those cliffs to the top of Table Mountain. But I've heard of nobody who has tried that and returned to talk about it."

Chapter 3

"I'm against it and begging you not to go," Faith insisted in Swahili, tears of fear pooling in her eyes. "And if you do go, I will not stay here."

"Impossible for you to come along. The path is steep and the bush thick, my dove."

"There are leopards on this mountain," Faith bargained. "The white man said that they hunt the livestock on the fringes of the town."

"If they are there, then they are here too," Chikunda countered, "and we have thus far been safe."

"Well, I'm not staying here," she emphasized.

"There is nowhere else for you," Chikunda pointed out.

"I don't see why you would want to go. What is there to see? There is no point."

"I need to estimate the magnitude of the challenge that we face, dove. That mountain is bigger than it looks, the distances wider, the going worse."

"This man," she indicated toward Sebastião, "says it is dangerous… this notion of yours and the trip you expect us to do."

"By all means, speak in private," Sebastião suggested in Portuguese, "but if you point to me and talk about me in my presence… perhaps consider it a little rude."

There was a brittle edge to the bachelor's voice, as if they were nearing the end of their welcome. Or perhaps it was, as he hinted, a cultural affront to whisper secrets.

"I am sorry," Faith admitted timidly in Portuguese, and squeezed past the cupboard and through the fissure into the dwelling cave beyond.

"Are you still intent on this?" the cobbler quizzed Chikunda, easily guessing what the heated debate had been about.

"If you were me?"

"I'd do it, yes. You really have no option, you can't begin this journey blind, and you must begin it soon. But I do understand her disquiet too," Sebastião waved toward the dark cave where Faith had disappeared.

"It is stressful."

"She's worried about me? About being left alone with me?"

"No. That's not why she pointed to you. She pointed out that even you said it was dangerous. To go scouting."

"Aye… but necessary too," Sebastião agreed. "And, yes, I'm a stranger. It will take you a full day to complete for sure. I can leave her here alone and busy myself if it pleases her. I have errands to run. She can hole up in there."

"I'd be more comfortable if you remained," Chikunda admitted.

"Well…" he huffed. "I could do both. I'm in need of more seafood for dinner, eggs and a pail of milk. I could busy myself for half the day with these things. When are you thinking of going?"

"Tomorrow," Chikunda proposed.

Sebastião whistled through his teeth. "You felt the hot wind of today and saw the crown of cloud on the mountain just now?" He waved vaguely up and behind the hovel, indicating toward the crest of the mountain. "When that lion's head wears a mane of cloud, we have two days of rain ahead. The mountain can be treacherous when it's under a blanket."

"I can move cautiously… get out at first light."

"And the town will be socked in anyway. You won't see much."

"The weather here seems to come in waves. It should clear enough to give me a glimpse and some bearings."

"It should," Sebastião agreed.

"Can you harvest shellfish when the weather turns?"

"If you know where to look," the genial Portuguese nodded.

"Where's the path?" Chikunda ducked outside.

Sebastião followed him.

"Pretty straightforward. Get off this track as soon as you can, a few hundred paces up this road past where we sat. Aim for that outcrop of boulders there, you'll find the game path." He pointed to the skyline of the ridge where a boulder field stood on the saddle of a ridge.

It looked to be perhaps half a mile of slog.

"The bush is thick and full of thistle, best you use my leather leggings or you'll be torn to shreds. And you're in luck—I'm a cobbler, of course." He dug in a well-worn chest and produced a set of fine-looking boots. "Fixed them for a man, but he accepted the wrong duel before he could return for them."

"Thank you." Chikunda took them. "They may fit. And beyond that ridge?"

"You'll see when you're there, it's obvious. The saddle of that ridge extends to the north. Once you're at the top, follow it. The whole plan of the town will be set below you. Take care, particularly of snakes at this time of year."

"Venomous ones?"

"Cobras, adders… puff adders."

"What do adders look like? Are they dangerous?"

The Portuguese rolled his eyes.

"Long as my arm, but much thicker. Diamond pattern, diamond-shaped head. You don't want to get bitten."

It was still in the black of night and under a drizzling cloak of miserable rain when Chikunda kissed his bride goodbye and stepped out into the dark, moving quickly out of earshot of her tearful protestations.

Second-guessing the wisdom of his trek, he hardened his heart against the pull to be back inside the claustrophobic cave under the stinking blanket, holding the most precious thing in his life to his chest.

He heard Jack's excited barks fade as he made his way north on the path past the granite lookout where he had sat learning from the cobbler.

Eventually, his eyes adjusted to the starless dark of a cloudy pre-dawn and he stumbled less.

Four hundred slippery paces he counted from when the path flattened out from its slow ascent, and he groped for the entrance to the footpath that would take him straight up the mountain.

The Portuguese had said it would be just after the path turned sharp left on its final straightaway to the bluff and out of sight beyond.

After two false attempts, one pathway blocked by thick bush and another by a cavernous water-cut channel, he found the access point and began the laborious climb.

By the time he made the saddle of the ridge, night had given its reluctant way to an insipid dawn.

He stopped to catch his breath and to tend a minor twist to his ankle.

The drizzle stopped a while giving him a near vertical view down over the bay that had been his landing site on this tip of the continent.

His eyes were drawn to the distant ridge that punched its granite fist out into the Atlantic, drawing a southern boundary to the bay of Schoenmakers Gat. Right down below him were those last bones of his shipwreck and out beyond the ridge was the tangle of a rocky promenade that had been his temporary haven for two months.

Baai van von Kamptz was out of sight from this vantage point.

He turned his back on it all and began to bushwhack toward the skyline of ridge.

The towering grey rock cliffs of the lion's head mountain still soared high above even at this great elevation. Closer to them now, he could see vast slab faces with vertical fractures cutting the horizontal strata and other scars the mountain must have gathered with great age.

His natural curiosity drew him to climb further, to introduce himself to this part of the continent, to slap those old buttresses as he would a good friend on the back. A good friend that had halted his miserable kidnapping and passage to another more distant foreign land from which there would certainly be no hope of return.

Instead, from that ridge still ahead he would see Africa proper again in all its breadth and majesty. The cobbler had promised that if the weather cleared, he would see thirty or more miles across the plain called the Cape Flats—a vast stretch of beach sand—to a horizon-wide rack of blue mountains in the hazy distance.

The thought of the land under his feet still being his Africa kept him trudging along, dreaming of home with each step.

The sun was shy today, briefly peeking out for a few moments between the curtains of low and weeping fog, the bush he was pushing through wet with its tears.

At noon, somewhere below his elevation, Chikunda heard the BOOM of the naval gun placed above the town on this signaling hill. The cobbler had told him to expect the sound of this newly installed mechanism designed to warn the townsfolk and ships' crews at anchor in the bay that the noon zenith had been reached and the afternoon was beginning to waste.

In this drab light and under these miserable circumstances, the little town huddling below the vast flat-topped mountain to his right looked forlorn. But Chikunda was a man of great optimism and he saw past the bitterness of his predicament to estimate how magnificently it might present itself when the sky stretched in aching blue and the birds came out to welcome a happier day.

He stopped and allowed himself to swig from the flask that the Portuguese had loaned to him and nibble unhappily on an unpleasantly furry, tasteless little biscuit.

He took in the town through the spyglass that the shoemaker had recommended he carry. A handful of houses stood on a grid of roads that were centred on a walled-off fort with foundations sunk into the beach. Spring tide was in and a wave surge was driven by the passing weather front, causing the water to lap against one of the fort's buttress walls.

The fort's footprint had a five-pointed star design with tall battlements hewn from locally quarried stone. The white cement and square blocks of rock construction gave the edifice the look of a low, squat tortoise. Offspring buildings ate the natural dunes and scrub of the bay with relentless slowness and digested them into regimented rows and columns of European order.

Small as it was, the fort looked formidable.

It took him almost the rest of the day to reach the next prominent position at the northernmost end of the mountain's saddle.

Even from halfway to this point, he could have turned back; he'd seen enough. He'd already spied those fabled mountains of promise in the far distance.

Instead, he'd kept going, pretending to himself that he needed the best possible sense of what lay ahead when or *if* he and Faith ever made it southward past the garrison at Baai van von Kamptz, along the coast via the wooded fishing bay, its valley leading to the small mountain pass and perhaps on to freedom in the distant mountains.

In truth, he knew the real reason he'd pressed on was the mention of his nemesis, the cruel bosun aboard the slaver, Alfonso Oliveira. Something sliding through Chikunda's gut since he'd heard that name again had kept him driving onward—a peculiar compulsion to look down onto the grisly apparatus at Gallows Hill, which was evidently this man's lair. The horror of fascination kept him accelerating onward as the sun slowly sank through the heavens.

But the vantage point he'd hoped to find for this purpose was an elusive beast.

Each time he set his eyes on the point he must reach to secure the view, he arrived there to find it to be a false promise. From each new vantage point, he would realize the real location that would afford him a sighting, and it always lay a short, tantalizing distance ahead.

Far out in the middle of the large bay lay an island. The cobbler had said it was good hunting grounds for seals, or *robbe* in Dutch. They called it Robben Island, a place of banishment for misdemeanours.

And so it was that when the weather began to clear in the late afternoon and the sun came out to direct its shimmering beam at Chikunda across the undulating grey-green ocean, the place of execution finally came into view.

There was not much there—nothing to see from this elevation even through the spyglass. Some wooden poles set into the ground and other timber structures atop a well-worn parade ground of sorts.

Nobody was about.

It hadn't been worth the effort and waste of precious time, and Chikunda cursed his own foolishness for having pressed on and on.

He'd made his approach to this point along the eastern flank of the signalling hill above the town.

Turning back to try and reach Faith before sunset, he took the more direct route, traversing the western side with the ocean at his right shoulder.

One last look over Table Bay where a dozen ships lay at anchor in the bay, the forbidding masts and spars, ropes and reefed sails sending shivers of memory through his whole body. The three weeks he'd spent on one of these creaking, stinking torture contraptions had scarred him for life. He felt only dread at their sight.

He turned away and began to move quickly, making easier progress on this arider stretch of the mountain.

Down below, a green common was spread around a flooded waterway and through the spy glass he saw two dirt tracks running parallel for the length of the coast, one near the water, the other closer to the slope.

Clutches of cattle grazed in various places, evidently not being tended.

The coastline beyond was rocky with no sign of beach for safe landing. The rock of this shore was black and angular, lying in rows of nearly military formation pointing from the shore to the sea.

It seemed curious to him that the rounded, light-coloured granite rock didn't exist here and the black angular rock found here didn't exist in the place he had been living not far distant.

Through some recent education at the Mission where he and Faith had met, his natural curiosity for all things strange and remarkable had been strummed.

These kinds of details—when one kind of rock became another, or why and how this might be—fixated his mind.

Most people he had met during his lifetime considered this sort of fascination with details to be a waste of time, and even Chikunda could not answer to himself why gathering knowledge mattered to him.

He now simply accepted that he was built this way and no longer questioned it.

The urge to witness this transition kept his eyes peeled to distinguish the point at which one sort of rock gave way to the other.

Now it was a race against the setting sun, inching as it was closer toward the horizon with every stride he made.

By the time the sun's leading edge touched the water, he was arriving level with the transition of the rocks on the coastline, but still frustratingly short of the ridge that would give him first sight of the bay of Schoenmakers Gat.

He doubled his efforts on now tiring legs. Once more, he silently thanked the cobbler for the use of his good shoes and leather leggings, while the thistle-like waist-high scrub repeatedly lashed his exposed arms until they were an itchy network of cat-scratches weeping blood.

It was a moonless night and the stars had appeared.

The radiance of the Milky Way provided the only light and barks from baboons and other animal sounds set Chikunda's nerves to jangling, unarmed and unable to defend himself if a prowling leopard was about.

Finally, stumbling and slipping, doubling back from dead-ends of bush or cervices cut by river washes and landslides into the mountain scree, he came over the brow of the last headland that gave him a view of the welcoming bay and his destination. The details were near impossible to distinguish by starlight alone.

The land pitched steeply. He began his descent on this final run, and that is when he saw the small crowd of fiery torches.

It stopped him dead in his tracks.

He studied it and saw that the lit throng was retreating, moving away from him, southward, along the contour path that he estimated the cobbler had led them on that first day heading north toward his cave.

Alarm bells were ringing in his head.

"It is rare that anyone passes this way. I go weeks without seeing a soul." The Portuguese's voice echoed in his head. He could taste the terror of what this portended and he accelerated, not knowing what he could do to alleviate the situation even if it proved to be the worst-case scenario.

Every conceivable possibility crowded his mind. *Lost travellers? Fishermen? Customers of the shoemaker....? An ordinary patrol, perhaps?*

And at that instant, the ground gave way beneath his feet, and he went with it down into the pitch-blackness like a hooded man falling through the executioner's trapdoor.

Chapter 4

Chikunda awoke to naked agony.

The ankle he'd twisted at the start of the day was exploding with a searing pain so ferocious that he could scarcely believe a man could suffer it and still live.

He ran his hand down his leg and shin, expecting to feel the jagged bone jutting from tattered flesh. Instead, there was a bulbous swelling of a burning hot mound where his ankle should be that wobbled like a jellyfish.

He tried to adjust his position and a convulsion of new sparks from the distended limb drove his mind into new territories of torment.

He whooped with the pain of it, hot tears in his eyes.

And then the memory of why he was here and what he'd seen the moment before the fall came crashing in on him like the embankments of the trickling river he was lying in.

"Mkiwa!" he started to sob, repeating the Swahili name of his wife somewhere out there in the night, most likely being ushered away by the torches. Or—the optimist in him fought back—safely hidden in the cave not far away.

The truth of where she was presently was a gamble and flip of a coin. A fact already set by destiny but unknown to Chikunda, and the knowledge of this dichotomy teased him back and forth as he tried to roll to a better position and understand whether there was a way out.

But, there was nothing he could do.

It was too dark down in the ditch, too steep on either side, and the course of the river was hemmed in by matted bush.

So there Chikunda lay and he began to weep. For his circumstance, for his pain, and for the outcome of his wife's well-being that was already set.

Hours dragged by and the only visible thing, the stars in a narrow band of sky above, crept slowly along in the sky above.

The only comfort Chikunda could find was by elevating that ankle up the embankment he had fallen down. This put his head and shoulders into the icy slosh of the rivulet that had steadily cut this course he was trapped in.

Finally, the bird songs began and the land above him showed the first blush of dawn creeping in.

As the stars gave way to the pale morning light, he began to see his way out of the water-cut crevasse.

The sides of it were taller than he stood by twice his height, but downstream the course seemed open. Just a dry dead thicket of bush plugged his route out of the tight valley.

Preparing himself for the onslaught of pain it would cost him to make his escape; he laid his swollen ankle into the numbing cold of the stream. Very slowly some relief washed over him, but his anguish about what he might find when he reached the cobbler's cave was now at a fever pitch and he found himself whimpering again, not even from the pain but from the fear of an unknown reality.

The surf was running angry and savage, monstrous waves curling in slow motion on the outer reefs far below the path. Yet, the sky was clear and achingly blue as Chikunda hobbled down the path, dragging his swollen ankle on a makeshift branch that he used as a crutch to prop up his right side.

It was slow going over the rough track, but Chikunda made the best time possible. He passed the path by which he'd accessed the mountain more than twenty-four hours earlier, then the descent began and he passed the granite boulder on which he'd sat with the cobbler, discussing the wreck.

He was now in hailing distance of the cave, but he quelled the urge to shout out—the scream that leapt to his throat, ready to beg for help in walking and relief from his worst fears.

As he drew closer, the first sign that something was very wrong struck him like a gong to the temple. The lean-to structure at the mouth of the cave was ripped down and lying to one side.

Chikunda began to hop, wincing with each step, agony exploding in his brain.

But his brain barely registered the affront as reality threatened the worst possible outcome.

He reached the mouth of the cave and called into it urgently, sweat from pain and fear streaming down his temples.

Inside was bedlam, the cupboard pulled down, the table overturned, the bed thrown across the room.

The floor was strewn with the flotsam of the cobbler's life, broken pottery and treasures from the sleeping cave he'd shared with Faith emptied into the main cave.

Chikunda found himself crying and repeating Faith's Swahili name over and over in a mantra of manic desperation, as if the spell could wind back time.

The situation was obvious—the blunderbuss not on its hook above the door and Jack nowhere to be seen.

What to do next? What? How?!

The questions detonated in his head, sending devastating waves of terror racing around his body.

He limped out of the cave and called urgently into the valley up behind the cave, and only the morning chorus of birds was heard in reply.

He dragged his leg to the other side of the path to call down the valley, and the low rumble of the surf echoed back.

He was alone in the dungeon of his fear on this exposed mountain face in a foreign land. The weight of his predicament came crashing down like an avalanche descending from the peak way above, and his cries turned to sobs. And then the sobs gave way to soundless, wracking convulsions. The convulsions grew into animal howls that ricocheted around and around in his mind, tormenting him till he felt he could take no more. Were the cliff at this point steep enough or the blunderbuss available, he knew that this was the moment that he would end it all.

It was then that he remembered the gleaming steel weapons wrapped in canvass within the rear sleeping chamber of the cave.

He limped inside, pushing through the clutter, wondering what he'd do with the swords if he found them. It was a question the blind panic of the moment could not answer, as the raw instinct of the warrior began to surface.

While he searched, his mind played tricks on him—Faith's tinkling voice emerging from the drips at the back of the cave, the occasional birdcall becoming his name in her tone.

Madness overtook him, and the swords were nowhere to be found.

They'd taken them, whoever *they* were.

They would be the garrison, the soldiers… or the Bosun's search party.

They would have gone back to the town, to the five-pointed star fort he had looked down onto.

Chikunda gave up and retreated from the cave.

Out in the dirt at the doorway, not knowing which way to turn, he slumped to the earth and sobbed some more, imagining the worst that his wife was enduring at this moment.

Had the Portuguese turned her in? For a reward? *Impossible!* he thought.

Had the man pursued his promise and distanced himself from harbouring the runaway woman? Had he told the assailants which way Chikunda had gone?

All impossible questions to answer.

He would get up now and walk into town and give himself up. There was no alternative.

Knowing these strangers as he already did from his Arab captors and the cruelties aboard the ship that had brought him here, he would no doubt take a lashing for this at the very least, but perhaps they would be lenient.

Perhaps these people would yet have clemency. They were British, after all. Surely, they would see that his wife was pregnant and allow them to pass. Was it madness to think this way?

He didn't know, but he also couldn't tame his rampaging mind.

Hadn't the Portuguese also said that the Dutch executioner couldn't stomach the treatment that the English dished out?

He started to laugh now, laugh and sob. It was insanity overtaking him. He was sliding into the spirit world of possession and he knew it.

There, amid the mess, lying in the dirt was the biscuit tin and the last of its furry contents.

It had been a full day since Chikunda had eaten a meagre meal and more from a voice of deduction at the very back of his mind than hunger's urging, he picked one up and put it joylessly into his mouth.

He began to chew.

It was the opening of a sluice as he swallowed that first mean mouthful. Ravenous hunger came upon him like a flood.

With both hands, he began to feed his mouth, the biscuits tasting better and better after the ravages to his depleted body.

As the sustenance hit his stomach and began to surge into his bloodstream, the fog of despair also began to lift.

Now is the time for a cool and calculating head, the hermit who lived in this cave repeated in Chikunda's head.

"Now is the time for a cool head," he repeated to himself aloud.

There would be better food, he reminded himself. The shoemaker had gone to harvest.

Into the cave he went, even his foot improving with the lift of his mood.

He couldn't put weight on it, but he had learned now to lock his ankle and walk only on his heel.

He dropped to his knees and felt under the ledge where the icy drip-drip-drip kept the hessian cover over the lobster saturated.

Through the fabric, he could feel the knobbed and pointy armour of the two heavy beasts wrapped within and another odd shape.

The two spiny lobsters were still very much alive, flapping and clapping their wide red tails up against their chests, eight legs spread so wide they could span Chikunda's chest, each leg thicker than his thumb. The other item was a tortoise—a *skilpad* as the cobbler had called it—its head removed.

One cooked lobster would be more than enough for a meal.

If they came for him while he cooked it, so be it; he resigned himself to fate.

There seemed no point in rushing now, since rushing was barely a crawling speed anyway.

Right now, he must eat—eat and think.

Having eaten most of the sweet flesh, Chikunda's optimism bounced back.

He stowed the other lobster and tortoise, and wrapped the remaining cooked flesh to eat later or take with him.

This moment felt very familiar, an echo of that first terrifying sight of the slaver as the cutter that had carried Faith and him out from the shore bumped up against the hull of the schooner *São José de Afrika*.

That moment had been almost three months ago. His strategy then had been to identify the

InDuna—the headman—of that wooden vessel and become indispensable to him.

As he'd told the Portuguese, it hadn't worked out precisely that way, but it had worked out nearly as well. He'd won the Captain's protection but riled the Bosun to torture his mind when his body was put off limits.

It had kept them out of the holds, a turn of good fortune that certainly spared their lives when the ship had wrecked.

And now the need to identify and appeal to another InDuna, to the Chief at the stone fort in the town, seemed likely to be upon Chikunda once again.

Armed with the knowledge that his Christianity might be his shield in this British colony, his mind cleared and the path of options before him focused on that supreme turn of fate that could win him his freedom. His mind already began to work on the possibilities of how to earn a passage back up the coast to his home in Portuguese Mozambique.

With his mind once more buoyed and sharp, it struck him that the little lip overhang where the lobster were stored might be duplicated elsewhere in the rear cave.

He limped back inside and began to crawl in the gloom, feeling for a recess… and there he found it. Instantly his hand fell on the stiff canvas wrapping.

He brought the bundle out, and between its layers he felt the distinct shape and fluid curve of those magnificent weapons.

What to do now?

His mind cartwheeled for an answer.

It had been an instinct to lay his hands on the weapon, but having found them, these were not his possessions and he had no right to them, even in this dire situation.

He held them to his chest and prayed for the answer. They were an insurance policy, but not *his* insurance policy.

Even if they were, and he walked into town carrying them, they would be forfeit or he would be dead—that was the answer to his prayers.

Re-stow them.

So, he did.

Now with a plan, nuance of execution needed to be considered. He needed to play it out on his terms.

He needed to walk into the town of his own volition, to surrender himself to the chief personally, if possible.

He couldn't afford to be trapped here in this cave, cowering and dragged from it like a common criminal on the run, then taken in for reward.

This was now a mind game. He could no longer believe himself to be on the run.

But the time wasn't right yet to surrender himself.

Whether he went into custody today or in three days' time would have no effect on improving Faith's lot, but it would allow him to walk proudly and surely and try to identify where or how to target the man in charge.

His mind crisp and clear with objectives, he dared not risk being trapped now, and he dared not be caught on the roads. From here on out, he would only be venturing where nobody else would, off the beaten track and below the skyline.

He went back into the cave and began selecting survival items that wouldn't impair the Portuguese's lifestyle if he returned.

Then he began the arduous effort of backtracking the path up the mountain that he'd taken in the dark and the rain.

Chapter 5

In the bush, overlooking the most deserted part of the coast that he had seen during his circuit a day earlier, he made camp in a small crawlspace under the overhang of a granite rock.

The location was a watershed promontory that gave him two views within paces of each other.

One lookout was south, over Schoenmakers Gat bay and the path the cobbler had led them along from their original camp. The other was north, above the junction of the white and dark rocks and over the plain where cattle grazed in the very far distance.

He set out the survival kit he'd salvaged from the wreckage of the cobbler's cave and cleared a space big enough for a small fire that he'd make when the time was right.

While engaged in these small and painful preparations, he heard a sound—movement through the bush, footfalls, something traveling fast, closing in on him from below, following the path he'd shoved through the thicket.

He picked up the machete and readied himself to defend as best he could against whatever it was that was tracking him.

A branch in the bush shivered, betraying whatever it was approaching inbound through its lower reaches, and there was a flash of colour through the foliage, of fawn brown, and then Chikunda heard the sniffing.

It was a dog trailing him. An instant later he realized it was Jack, the hound's snout to the ground tracing Chikunda's path.

Jack saw him at the same instant and flew forward in two bounds, hitting Chikunda in the chest, knocking him over his injured ankle.

"Damn it, you fool," Chikunda scolded him, the improving ankle sending lightning bolts of pain piercing into his brain.

But the dog on top of him frantically licking his face made him laugh as his arms folded around the animal, partly to stop him, and partly to hear if there were perhaps footsteps following.

With that warm body to his chest, Chikunda's laughter turned to tears and then to sobs once more. Sobs at having something living that cared about him, something that, through its desperate whimpers and excited relief evidently needed care.

"Where are they boy? Your master? My Faith? Where have they gone?"

The stupid questions brought fresh tears as his own words distilled into his brain, becoming crystalized reality of circumstance.

"Where…?" he kept repeating between the sobs, "where?"

Chikunda inspected the dog. It had lost a dewclaw and its pads were badly tattered. Evidently it had been running unaccustomed distances over rough ground.

The evidence was coming together. The torches on the path, the ransacked cave and now the dog's trail-weary appearance. It suggested that the dog had trailed its master to a point it could follow no further, and then it had run home, and perhaps back again.

It had certainly then picked up the trail of the next closest ally, the most recent lodger at that cave, Chikunda.

Chikunda wanted to tend the hound's paws, but he knew not how. Jack, too, was frantic in his perpetual search, his ears swivelling towards the slope and back behind him.

Away he charged on a descent through the bushes, on an errand only his ears had detected.

Was this meaningful? Chikunda asked himself.

Should he follow or flee?

Was the dog here to tell him to return to the cave, to tell him that all was restored and well?

Was it abandoned and trying to find a friend but second-guessing itself?

Was it warning of a posse giving chase?

Where one dog had found him, another could also pursue.

What if Alfonso, the Bosun had a dog?

No doubt the Bosun now had Faith in his clutches or was influencing whoever did have her.

And that man certainly had ways of discovering which way her husband had gone.

Where was safe?

Chikunda needed another day—maybe two— to approach the town and the fort over this ridge. He'd probably close the final distance by night, to manage as few intermediaries between himself and the headman as was possible.

Jack was gone long enough to have galloped to the cave and back.

Right on cue, the dog reappeared panting furiously, his young belly pumping like bellows.

"Slow down boy," Chikunda cautioned him. "Come sit."

But the animal was on hot coals.

Down the track he went again, but was back in a briefer length of time, his wincing in pain unceasing. Pain from his damaged body, certainly, but also the agony of loss deep within, and Chikunda felt the same, too.

"It's okay, boy. We'll find your boss soon enough."

The dog's ears pricked up and he almost seemed to nod acknowledgement.

Off he scampered to the southward view, where he sat attentive as a statue, only his ears cupping every fragment of sound from every direction, and his eyes trying to shorten the distance.

Down the embankment he trotted, then back up and off to the southerly lookout in a frantic pattern of angst.

The dog's persistence with loyal attention delivered pangs of shame to Chikunda's mind. He felt that he should match the animal's passion with his own panicked haste to be reunited with his wife and save her from whatever fate...

The thought of it sickened him.

"Now is the time for a cool head," he reminded himself aloud and nodded his thanks inwardly to the shoemaker for capturing such good advice into such a crisp reminder.

The plan needed to unfold deliberately.

Chikunda woke in the dark, the warm body of his wife in his arms. His right arm pinned under it complaining of pins and numb deadness.

But the smell in his nostrils an instant later reminded him of the truth. This was Jack, snuggled under the rock overhang for warmth and comfort.

The relief of having Faith back and then the lie plucked from his reality all in the same instant plunged Chikunda's emotions off an emotional cliff. She was gone, Faith was another man's prisoner. Not very far away, but very far out of his reach.

He started to sob again into the dog's coat, and Jack reciprocated, licking his head.

When dawn came, Chikunda ate another of the lobster that he'd cooked the night before.

Jack sat watching silently, his head canted over askance, drool hanging from his mouth in long clear strands.

Chikunda huffed. This was precious nutrition that had to last him until... well, until he was captured, most likely.

"Here," he tossed the Jack the carapace with the feathery gill and other organs of the innards still attached.

Jack devoured it with crunching delight, swallowing the gloopy green and yellow body parts with relish.

"You're a good boy." Chikunda patted the dog's head and huffed. The dog lay his head on Chikunda's foot as if to impose no more plea on the man's limited rations.

"But what to do with you?" Chikunda asked.

"Is your boss back? And my wife? How will we know?"

The dog's eyes looked mournful, as if he understood.

"Did they go to town? Did men take them, boy?"

The dog sighed heavily as if to answer.

"You can't stay with me boy. I don't have food for the both of us, and where I'm going, you can't come."

Jack got up and went to the southern viewpoint.

"I'm going to have to get going." Chikunda had been massaging his own injured ankle, sensing that there was healing in practice—a moving of whatever made up that angry yellow and black bruising pattern that was laced all over the swollen limb.

He battled to his feet with small involuntary yelps and Jack's ears focused on him for a moment, but the dog's eyes never left the direction toward the path that led to the cave.

Chikunda began to lash the few possessions he had together with twine so that he could loop it over his shoulder and continue the battle against the slope with his makeshift crutch.

Something in Jack's whiny sound changed.

Chikunda looked up from his final preparations.

The dog was standing, trembling, his eyes and ears straining towards something far in the distance.

Cautiously, Chikunda limped forward.

There they were, a band of five men.

Black boots, white breeches, red tunics and the white slash of bandoliers across their chests. Felt hats bragging wildly of an empire.

One was on horseback and four were bearing long barrels pointing at the sky high above their shoulders.

They were on the cave path moving steadily northward toward the cave and on to his position.

Their presence spoke volumes about what had transpired. It confirmed there had been unusual activity. It obviously betokened that the regiment was backtracking to see if the one who had slipped through their net twice had returned.

On impulse, Chikunda ducked back below their line of sight.

What to do?

To run, or limp, as best he could higher and further away?

No.

Time for a cool head!

Stay.

Movement would draw attention.

Jack got up and made to gallop down the slope.

"No! No Jack! Sit… quiet…!" But the dog was beside himself with excitement.

He slipped from Chikunda's grasp and was gone, the sounds of his headlong plunge away down the slope and toward the contour path that the soldiers were making their way along melting into silence with the exception of the distant ocean below and birdsong.

Now what?

What calamity would the dog direct back to him? Would it reach them, not find its master, and give them the clue by charging back to his position?

If he got up to move, it would only track him once more by scent.

The smart move was to stay put.

Time moved like tree sap. Every small sound jangled Chikunda's nerves, every movement in the bush below set his heart on fire.

After an excruciating wait, while the sun clawed its way toward the zenith, the bush below started to tremble, and up came Jack, his pads torn anew from the exuberance of his departure.

"What, Jack… did you leave them? Are you leading them to me?" Chikunda asked of the dog, feeling fate with its icy grip once more about to rip his flimsy plans asunder.

The dog came to lie down looking defeated and scolded, its head hanging low, its eyes swimming with loss.

"Boy?" Chikunda asked warmly and Jack lay his chin on crossed front paws, his eyes blank.

"Where are the men?"

Chikunda had the spyglass ready and with a wash of relief he counted four on foot and one mounted soldier retreating down the path carrying with them odds and ends.

Carrying odds and ends?

What could this mean?

It couldn't be good. That Jack had returned meant Sebastião was still absent. The timing of the dog leaving and returning and the soldiers coming and going, carrying goods meant one thing and one thing only—they had intersected at the cave, and the dog had been driven off. The soldiers were on a mission and they were leaving with the objective of their efforts completed.

The whereabouts of Sebastião and Faith was clear now too—the answer to that question now painfully obvious.

A tear left Chikunda's eye and raced down his cheek. He mopped it away. This was not the time to be sentimental. It was the time to plan and be precise.

He hefted his small survival kit onto his shoulder and wondered for a brief moment if he should chance going back for those swords, but decided against it.

"Okay, go… Get out… AWAY!" he scolded Jack. The dog jumped up, confusion in his eyes. "Go on, off with you! You can't stay with me. I don't have food and you'll give me away at the sight of strangers."

The dog skulked out of range of any potential abuse from the castigating man, his head and tail sunk to new lows, the whites of his now bewildered eyes half-moons.

Chikunda turned his back on this stinging betrayal that fate had forced him to make, his gut twisting at it.

He hobbled diagonally along the slope, gaining altitude slowly, making for the distant skyline of the saddle he must traverse.

After ten paces, he turned to check and Jack was five paces behind him, the hound maintaining a stance of readiness to bolt in retreat.

"Go on Jack…" He could not pretend at anger again. "Go on, get away. Back to your cave." The dog halted and backed away half a pace. "Move it!"

It looked as if the dog might at least remain and not follow, so Chikunda turned and counted twenty paces, then turned again and found Jack still five paces behind him.

Jack backed up a half a pace.

"There is nothing I can do for you Jack. Follow me to the town and you'll be abandoned. Push off… GO!"

The dog turned and walked away slowly, his body howling grief and a broken heart.

Tears were in Chikunda's eyes as he turned back to continue the arduous trek into slavery.

He didn't look back again. He forced himself to look only ahead.

The noon cannon had long since reported the sun at its maximum.

Perhaps two thousand more hopping paces through the bush had brought Chikunda onto the ridge, and the little town beside the bay with the fort dipping its toes onto the beach emerged into view.

It was a glorious sight—just as Chikunda had imagined it might look when the sky was blue and the light played golden hues on the tall slab of Table Mountain.

It was only then that Chikunda allowed himself to look back, and there, five paces behind him slunk the dog. It immediately spun around to retreat two paces.

Chikunda sank down from exhaustion—fatigue of body but mostly of soul.

"Come here boy," he relented, and raised his arm in an arc. The dog trotted in with his head still low but his tail recovering.

Jack pushed in under Chikunda's armpit and his tears began to flood out of his eyes once more.

"You have to stop this, Jack. You have to stop doing this. You can do me no good and I can do nothing for you."

The dog licked his face, washing the tears away.

Chikunda put his arm about the dog's shoulders and the two of them sat, unlikely friends, gazing out over the vista of beauty that contained so much ugliness within its heart. Down below, somewhere, were the loves of their lives.

A cutter was being rowed out to one of the ships at anchor just off the shore.

Chikunda watched it pull up alongside and through the spyglass, he saw redcoats flanking a man with lanky black hair and it made his stomach turn. Many men had long black hair, he reminded himself.

The man was bundled up over the side, and something sickly slid through Chikunda's gut.

"You should go back, boy," he told the dog. "God knows, I would if I could. That place holds nothing for you and only one thing for me."

To his right, the soaring three-thousand-foot rampart that was Table Mountain made an amphitheatre, and Cape Town languished there on its stage.

As he watched, the shadow cast by the signalling hill where he was encamped began to tickle the fringe of the town, and though it was a warm evening, Chikunda felt ice cold, both within and without.

As dusk crept in, the two feathery wisps of smoke that had been rising at separate points high up among the rocks of the mountain gave way to twinkles of light that confirmed they were campfires.

Chikunda peered again through his spyglass and interpreted the sporadic dimming and re-ignition of those lights to be people moving about them.

Who could they be, he wondered?

The answer was more than rhetorical—it would be a crystal ball into his own future and how to plot its trajectory at this critical juncture of decision.

Were these renegades? Runaways like him? Or, soldiers patrolling there to prevent them?

If the latter, were there more below him?

There was no way of telling.

The stars slowly awoke, the familiar Southern Cross up above the mountain and the unfaltering rash of the Milky Way, a slash in the roof of the sky.

In the best of times, these unchanging beacons always raised melancholy within Chikunda.

In melancholic times like this, they threatened to raise much worse.

Looking at the stars always took him back to his childhood and his father pointing to them as campfires of his ancestors looking down on him. They were a time machine that could pluck him out of his miserable circumstance, but not relieve him of the anguish that had increasingly stalked him with nothing but pain and loss during the last two seasons.

He sat now with only hours of dangerous freedom left, slowly dripping to their end.

By the time the sun rose, he would be a prisoner once more, probably within that stone fort that now had torches lit above its battlements and ghostly activity visible in the murky light that they effused.

Somewhere within the range of his sight was his Faith and his unborn child.

Would it be too much, he asked of his ancestors at their encampments looking down, if they saw to it that the place of her capture might somehow be illuminated?

Would this small miracle be granted by the Christian God to whom he had given himself so fully?

Could no ray simply shine down and allow him one last fleeting chance to find his wife? To abscond away with her into the depths of his own dark continent out there, and take his chances with nature away from these savage strangers?

Jack felt the heavy blanket of despair too, the sighing whistle of periodic exhalations reciting his own sad tale.

The dog lay with his paws pointed toward the town but his snout crossed toward his left, toward Chikunda and the ocean, as though there was something out there that he longed for.

Eventually, Chikunda stood, and Jack rose too.

Through the long night, the pair picked their way slowly down.

The sliver of moon provided just enough light to see by.

Leaves of a wild tobacco plant that Chikunda had bandaged to his injured ankle the night before had worked wonders. He could put no force into a thrust off that leg, but he could now at least get his full weight onto the heel if he did so cautiously.

Long before the sun began to blush the eastern horizon, Chikunda was already on the first manmade track through the arid dry bush at the mountain's lower slopes.

He crossed over a gutter carrying a trickle that must have once been a river.

He turned to Jack, feeling a rock in his heart as heavy as shot and as cold as the steel of those fine blades still hidden in the cobbler's cave.

"It's time to part, my boy," he patted the dog's head. "Off with you now!"

The dog detected the change in the man's hissing command. He receded a few paces, his ears matching his tail in a collapse of trust.

"Go on!" Chikunda scolded, keeping his voice low and urgent, "...go!"

He pretended to pick up a stone and the dog skulked out of range.

With tears coursing down his face, Chikunda turned from the last friend he had and began to limp towards the fort.

Down at sea level, the lay of the land changed character. Small sand dunes topped by reeds lay to his left—he still remembered how it must have been before the tracks and buildings had come to flatten and swallow them.

Over roads compacted by cart wheels and horse hooves that ran in a grid between low buildings, he made his way toward the fort, its buttress of stone walls looming taller and taller.

The sound of his feet softly sighing with each step and the waves gentle and languid on the beach over his left shoulder were the only sounds.

"HALT! Who goes there?" came the challenge from high above on the battlement.

Chikunda had prepared for this moment, for what he would say to a guard at the gate: a formal request to speak with the InDuna—the headman—about a serious and confidential matter.

He had not expected a public hailing contest overheard by any number of potential foes, with Jack lending voice to the confrontation.

"My name is Chikunda," he stammered in broken English, a language he could only relay a handful of words in before translating the next batch as best he could. "I have big problem must talk to top boss man of building."

"What do you want? Who are you? Who is your master?" the man called back, the white sash crossing diagonally over the dark red tunic giving the man vast authority.

Chikunda's English abandoned him under pressure.

"STAND WHERE YOU ARE!" the soldier ordered. "Guards!"

He began to frantically ring a bell.

Chikunda stood swaying, more from the unravelling situation than the exhaustion and lack of food during the last day of exertions.

He looked about himself, hopelessness overtaking him. Jack had retreated but was still barking some distance away.

The vast wooden slatted doors of the fort creaked open and a phalanx of uniformed men poured out brandishing long-barrelled smoothbores with bayonets affixed.

With ruthless, drilled efficiency, they encircled him.

"Get your hands on your head!" a man with a cruel mien to his voice shouted.

Chikunda understood only the tone, not the instruction, in the fear of that moment.

To enforce it, one of the men slammed the butt of his muzzle loader into Chikunda's kidneys, and everything went black.

When he awoke, Chikunda found himself on the icy dank floor of the cobbler's cave.

In the blackness, he rolled from his belly to his back but the pain of it made him whimper and roll back onto his face.

It felt like a huge, cold rock had been inserted through his flesh on that side and was chained to him. He felt in the dark as best he could and discovered the damp rock wall of the cave that he'd become accustomed to next to Faith.

But now the truth of his circumstance came trickling into his mind.

This wasn't the cave.

The rock in his back was the pulverized muscle and kidney where the musketeer had slammed him.

Every breath was a new agony so severe that his destroyed ankle evaporated to insignificance.

The old nightmare was upon him. The same icy manacles he'd worn from the instant the Arab slave traders had set upon him and Faith in their travels, the same chains his new Portuguese owners had exchanged for their own. The weight and clinking of them were a torture in themselves beyond any he'd ever imagined he'd meet in his life.

But they were the least of his troubles.

There were echoes within this chamber, echoes coming from beyond its walls. Metallic sounds of similar chains being dragged past. Rough voices spitting orders. The familiar whistle and schlock of a lash punctuating the instructions. The quavering howl of compliance. Heavy wood reverberating against stone doorways with the thunder of closure, attesting to the imprisonment.

There in the dark Chikunda lay, the theatre of his collapsing mind tortured with these things until he thought he may lose his wits altogether.

And when that point of despair was reached and surpassed, new layers of sorrow within him yawned open.

After an eternity of this passive torture, his chamber suddenly clattered with the sound of a bolt shot back and the rumble of its door thrown open.

Light streamed painfully in and an apparition stood there in relief against the glare.

"UP!" was all he understood from a guttural drumroll of instructions.

He tried to rise and was helped by a boot in the ribs.

Manhandled under each armpit, he was dragged down the echoing short corridor and into the fierce glare of the African sun.

Across a well-pounded dirt parade ground where soldiers, slaves and others toiled or went about their business.

His eyes slowly accustomed to the light as his feet tried as best they could to carry him and earn less painful encouragement from his guards who dragged him towards a whitewashed building with an elevated doorway and elaborate stairway.

Up and up he was yanked, step by bruising step, and slid into a vast hall with rich wall-hung tapestries and acres of lustrous timber flooring.

"So," announced a man with a drawn face and a complexion like death behind a vast desk as he looked up, laying the feather quill he was scribing with aside. "The prodigal returns."

Prodigal—it was one English word known to Chikunda.

The prodigal son returning. The lost welcomed without sanction by the authority figure, in spite of underlings calling for censure.

Through the fog of his agony, the use of that one word carried Chikunda's mind into a storm of hopeful confusion.

Was this man being literal or figurative? The answer to that question plotted two entirely opposite courses for how his life may play out.

"I…" Chikunda stammered, trying to find English words to respond with. "We have *be* tried to survive for our lives," he offered.

"You make no sense, boy," the old man grumbled just as a door opened into the room to one side of him and in glided a woman of majestic bearing.

The old man turned to her and his mournful face showed a wash of life.

"Jane my dear," his voice cooed with warmth and deference.

"Is this the slave? The runaway?" she inquired, a filament of concern in her tone.

"Yes, my dear. Limped up to the battlements this morning without fuss or ado."

"His face suggests discomfort." She came quickly to Chikunda, a maternal tenderness in her eye. "Do you understand English?" she asked directly.

"A little," Chikunda replied, quaking, reeling.

"Ma'am…!" The old man emphasized. "You always call a white woman Ma'am."

"I'm a little sorry, sire… Ma'am," Chikunda added. "I understand English but am badly talking."

"George," the woman implored, looking at the old man fiercely, "this man is in dreadful pain and anguish; we may forgo the formalities for the time being."

"As you please," the man said defensively, waving the guards out of earshot, evidently concerned that they not witness a further down dressing from the woman. "This is a fugitive from the law," he reminded the woman. "His sorry state is his own doing."

"His incarceration was evidently not," she snapped back, sinking her haunches for a closer look at the leg Chikunda favoured. "Did you twist it?" she asked the manacled man.

"Ma'am, yes. I in a fall."

"Can you kindly call the surgeon?" she requested of the old man.

He rolled his eyes and began to protest, but her withering look forestalled him and he indicated with a minute finger wave to one of the footmen to do the lady's bidding.

"Slave or no slave, George," she admonished in a matronly voice, "there is no need to suspend our humanity."

"There is also no need to expend his Majesty's finite resources unnecessarily," he grumbled, without lending it too much conviction.

"I would hardly call the inspection of an injury and perhaps its manipulation a vast expenditure of that pompous fool's bloated wealth," she chided.

"You speak of sedition easily, my dear. May you keep your head in spite of your highborn status."

"I am the wife of the Governor." The woman indicated the old man to Chikunda. "And we are, as you may have guessed, now the unfortunate overseers of this godforsaken piece of windswept land at the end of your continent. As I understand it, you are a survivor of the wreck? Of the slaver that went aground two months ago?"

"Ma'am, yes," Chikunda nodded. "My wife, Faith, and me… we are."

"Your wife? The woman taken into custody two days ago? Then you are her husband?"

"Her owner suggests otherwise," the old man pointed out, raising an eyebrow.

"That Portuguese pile of misery?" the woman responded. "You believe anything he says?"

"Over this… thing?" The old man waved the back of his hand toward Chikunda. "Well, yes. What other option? If the Bosun says that the woman was his woman, then I prefer his word."

The words slapped Chikunda like a hammer blow and he wondered if he had heard wrong.

"The squalid little man who hates everyone and most particularly blacks with such venom… the Bosun… you believe that *that* thing would also call the woman his wife and impregnate her, when she says quite the opposite? That the child in her belly is this man's child, and that now this man corroborates it himself?"

"This is not my squabble," the old man huffed in frustration. "In a few months, the wretched thing will be birthed and the truth will be known without doubt." He rose. "I have more pressing matters to deal with than the petty squabbles and claims and counterclaims of mercenaries and their property. I merely wanted to take a look at this impressive beast before we hand him over to his rightful owner. I am satisfied that he is in good health, and the Bosun or whatever he is can do with his own property as he pleases. Now if you would kindly excuse us. Jane, I think it is time for your attentions to be loaned to the master of the gardens, and my precious time to be applied to the running of this miserable little dump."

With that, he stood from his desk and disappeared through the same door that his wife had recently entered from.

"I'm sorry about my husband's attitude." The white woman, quite some years younger than the old man, spoke slowly and warmly to Chikunda. "Alas, he suffers an ulcer and constipation of the gut and it makes him far less, shall we say, agreeable, than he ought to be."

As she was speaking, a living nightmare came into view, rising like a volcano up the stairs outside.

Chikunda could not restrain his eyes from fixating on the demon now coming in through the door.

The lady followed Chikunda's shocked stare and turned to face the man.

Alfonso Oliveira, the boatswain—Bosun—had unmistakable proportions approximately similar to a stunted pig with no neck.

An exceedingly ugly man, he was built like a fortress with a bald head and a vein-infested nose that had an angry beetroot bulb at its end.

He took his duties far past boundaries of ferocity that even the British Navy's legendary brutally would allow.

Since last Chikunda had seen him, the man had developed a skin rash of sorts, open sores at his neckline and pocks on his skin.

Chikunda recognized the thing that hung from the man's hand; it was a scourge. It was a well-worn truss of black plaited leather cables, each periodically knobbed with knots along their length.

As long as Chikunda had known this man aboard the ship, this instrument of persuasion or a heavy club had perpetually swung from his grip. They were the tools of his trade.

"M'Lady," the Bosun growled to the woman in a thickly laced Portuguese accent, miming an exuberant bow and tip of a hat that he did not wear.

The woman looked him up and down with disgust, as if the man were a column of faeces brought to life.

"I have come to fetch my wretched property," he announced to the woman. "I am sorry if he has been cause for any distress to yourself."

"The surgeon will be here now," the woman spoke without looking at him, "to ensure that the man is fit enough to be released."

"Oh, he is fit," the Bosun guffawed, "fit enough for what I have in mind for him." He smiled with a bizarre air of camaraderie toward Chikunda as if they had been firm friends for a long time. "Besides, these animals are tough beyond imagining, m'lady. They are not human. Come on," he said to Chikunda, with a jerk of that boulder on his shoulders that was his head towards the door.

"He is very much human, I can assure you," she responded with haughty disdain, "and a surgeon for humans will first inspect him. I would be pleased if you would wait out of my sight."

The look the Bosun wore as he retreated down the stairs told Chikunda that a heavy debt would be levied for her words.

"I'm sorry," was all that the woman said.

In the minutes it took for the surgeon to arrive, Chikunda tried to explain that he was a baptized Christian and the woman nodded sagely.

"I will make these representations," she assured.

The surgeon was a thin, frail man with an Irish lilt to his high-pitched voice. He went about his duties with a light touch and an unusual sensibility.

"I believe that is a sprain. It needs strapping."

"Is there any way we can forestall the return of this poor man to that monster, James?" The lady inquired.

"He is rather emaciated, but I cannot say that it is sufficient grounds, I'm afraid."

There was something there, Chikunda recognized. Between the woman and this man. An affection and an essence of kindred spirit.

But more pressing than these idle speculations and the terror of presently being turned over as the personal property of a man with whom

Chikunda had a history and a debt that the master of the ship had amplified by interceding and forbidding the Bosun to visit his cruelties on the man—was the harrowing implication that the Bosun was claiming Faith as his own wife.

Chikunda spoke up.

"Ma'am," he addressed the woman in his halting English. "Much as my fear is makes me tremble to surrender to that man, I must go with haste to protect my wife."

The sincerity and menace in Chikunda's voice left the doctor and the woman speechless and silent.

"I understand," the woman said. "I can only wish you well in this, and assure you that I will work on my husband for a speedy resolution. I ask you to take care and not to make rash decisions." To the footman she instructed, "Kindly send that wretched man back up here before he leaves."

"There's no more I could do, I'm sorry Jane," Chikunda heard the doctor say as he was led clinking and clanking toward the African sun once more. "The small consolation is that the pox of syphilis is corroding that beastly man and we will soon enough be shod of him."

"My friend," the Bosun said in Portuguese, his hand on his prize possession's shoulder in a show of fondness for watching eyes. "I have been missing you, and it seems you make powerful friends very easily. But fear not, I have given the good lady my assurance that you will be treated with the most delicate of touch. She need not have bothered; I would do nothing to devalue such a prime hunk of meat that I own. Your body will remain unmarked, your mind however—what mind you might have—I cannot warrant will fare so well. Follow," he instructed, turning to walk slowly out through the fort's gates into the town. Chikunda did as best he could to keep pace on the strapped ankle.

When Jack approached with his tail thrashing and his emaciation from poor care starting to show, the Bosun hoofed the dog in its ribs as it passed him going to Chikunda. It yelped and ran like a hyena with its tail between its legs.

"Cursed thing," the Bosun spat into the dirt.

Chapter 6

"I'm very disappointed," the Bosun told Chikunda with menace in his voice and a smile on his face. "To hear such terrible lies spread so openly... Now, I have promised you and your protector that I will not harm even a hair on your very curly head. Alas, my friend, somebody must pay when you tell lies to the mistress. The Bible says that there must be retribution. Alas, this charitable feeling I have towards you I cannot say extends to the woman you call Faith." He paused dramatically. "That said, be a good man and bring for me the hippopotamus tail, it hangs on the hook third from left. Don't you know, it makes a most satisfying sound against naked flesh."

The Bosun had not mentioned Faith since he'd chained Chikunda by his throat collar to the ring set into the basement wall.

Chikunda had heard Faith's frightened voice cry out only once from one of the rooms upstairs. The sound of it had outrage and fear knitted into its pattern, and the Bosun's laugh that had followed—guttural and pitiless—had driven Chikunda to madness, slamming against his restraints, the steel collar bruising and tearing against his flesh.

"Off you go, be a good man. There is ample scope on that chain to do my bidding," he instructed Chikunda sweetly.

Chikunda remained sitting on the floor, his back against the wall and arms about his knees, his eyes fierce as a wildcat in the night.

"The whelp still has spirit, I see? Would you make me speak twice to you? My request was a simple one, the task well within your capacity."

Chikunda could not move, the hallucination of wrapping that restraining chain about the man's bull neck and strangling the life out of him dominating his mind.

The Bosun read it perfectly.

"You think yourself equal to me in strength, boy? Imagine that in your desperate condition you could take me on? I would welcome it, but I have work to do, work made harder by your dereliction of duty and refusing a command. What is there to do but add a little more to the tally for retribution?"

He stepped into the makeshift dungeon, keeping a wary eye on the black man coiled with fury like a spring. In his hand, instead of the perpetual whip, he carried his heavy club and he kept up the talking.

"…Suggesting to that good lady that you are a baptized Christian?" He laughed to emphasize his contempt. "It worked once with my foolish Captain. It kept you out of the holds alright. But the man was unlettered and did not understand the nuance of English law, he only guessed at it from chatter with other captains. He misinterpreted it. I'm sorry to tell you that the British will not misinterpret their own laws. I am in my full right to retain you as my personal property."

He lifted the rhino tail off its hook.

"They call it a *sjambok*," he told Chikunda. "Very effective in explaining matters." He wiggled the stiff hide and its tip cut the air with a *whirr*.

Chikunda sat paralyzed. His instinct to leap forward and rip the thing from the man's hands was overruled by his commitment to keep a cool clear head. It was trading a catastrophic situation over a wicked one.

"Oh, and your friend, the shoemaker? The deserter. I'm afraid his luck ran out in trying to save you. I delivered him to our Portuguese authorities and a merchant ship yesterday. He will be on his way to the mother country even as I speak, where his debt can be paid. That's a good boy," the Bosun commended, antagonizing his catatonic victim welded to the floor. "You're learning."

The door closed and Chikunda sat in the agony of waiting.

Before long, what sounded like gunshots rang out. The sound was forbidding.

Not long after the Bosun appeared with the lethal lash.

"I merely had your good woman oil it," he smirked. "I needed to test it, you see. There is work to do tomorrow. The *landros*—that is, the magistrate—he has promised us much exercise for your arm. Some bushman thieves they caught and he is considering the penalty now. You looked so concerned!" He smiled his awful amusement.

Chikunda did not answer. He could not answer, his mouth parched and his head cartwheeling as if it had been smashed with the club.

"You seem not to have the stomach for punishment being administered, my friend. This we must remedy. Did you think it was your woman receiving a thrashing?" He laughed an evil phlegm-lubricated chortle. "I cannot blame you. She deserved it for your lies, but let us mark it rather for a future occasion. Shall we tally…" he looked toward the heavens as if he was receiving the judgment from on high, "…three, no, five extra strokes when the inevitable day comes, eh?"

When he left, Chikunda collapsed from his seated position into a foetal pose. There he lay and dry heaved with vomit that refused to come. There was nothing in him. The stale bread crusts for his consumption thrown on the ground within his reach lay untouched.

Day dawned and the basement door creaked open.

"I have much exercise for you," the Bosun announced cheerfully. "Up you get. There is time only for a morning shit and then let's warm up that striking arm of yours. I don't want you injured. We have eight customers and a brisk walk ahead of us out to the Salt River where we deal with runaways and petty thieves. The good people of the town don't appreciate their ceaseless howls upsetting the gentry."

He came in and unhooked the sjambok.

"You'll be needing this," he said, and tossed it alongside Chikunda, his voice joyous.

He unlocked Chikunda's chain from its ring in the wall.

"Off with you to the ablutions, and don't loiter. I am giving you much freedom and I don't want to add to your woman's tally unnecessarily. She still has looks enough to fetch a decent price when the time comes."

He went out the door humming a sea shanty.

The cart with the eight small men chained to one another in it clattered and crashed over the poorly maintained road that ran toward the east of the fort.

Chikunda limped behind, forced to carry the sjambok for them to see.

The Bosun walked a few paces behind, chatting gaily with the jailer.

Tailing them was Jack.

They passed by a district of fishermen cottages set back from the dunes and beach.

"This is Woodstock," he called to Chikunda. "Mark it well, it is where I will require you to fetch me my meals from the fishmonger, over there, in that yonder house."

At the place of punishment, a single wooden pole was set into the ground and metal rings were pierced through it at different heights.

"Let us begin in the order that they are seated," the Bosun instructed. "It is as it was on the ship, either you do this properly and make your strikes in a manner that satisfies me, or for each weakness you show, we add it to your wife's tally. Understood? Begin then."

When the work was done and the wretches taken away near death's door, the Bosun sent Chikunda to wash the sjambok in the Salt River.

"The woman can oil it when we get home."

And then, seeing Chikunda broken in his spirits, the Bosun made a show of a special concession.

"You have done very well and I am proud of you. You may ride back on the cart. Shove those things aside to make way for my boy," he instructed the driver.

Jack found them on the return path and followed them at a distance, his eyes on Chikunda but always glancing at the Bosun.

And so it went, day in and day out. The smell of cooking, strange smells of piquant spices or delectable seafoods or fatty meats, all wafting down from the house or in from the street that the dungeon faced onto.

Eventually, Chikunda learned to eat the scraps thrown to him, sharing them with Jack who kept vigil in the street near the barred window.

Sitting in the dark sometimes for days on end with nothing to do, he would listen for his wife's angelic voice.

His mind often retreated to the certainty of his childhood on the coast where he would take a canoe out to sea each day to collect food for the family.

He remembered when he saw his wife for the first time; a more beautiful woman he had never known.

He followed her and discovered that she was an orphan living in a Catholic mission. In time, she was moved to another mission far away, and that was when he left home to follow her for days of travel southward.

After he had given himself to the Lord and they were married, it was on their return to his village to celebrate their union that they had been set upon by a rival tribe and sold to Arab slave traders.

The memories were bitter sweet and his idle mind in the dungeon basement became a workshop for the devil.

His only escape from these painful reflections was a drunk and outcast who had discovered him and would often sit on the street outside, sharing the gossip of the town in slurred speech to Chikunda.

From his stories, Chikunda learned that the smoke and fires he'd seen on the mountain above the town that last night of freedom were indeed runaways, perched in places up on the high cliffs that were not worth the effort of a punitive raid by the authorities. That the cobbler had indeed been captured and returned to Portugal. That a murder trial was about to commence for three mutinous sailors who murdered an officer. That the new English masters were disinterested in the plight of the mostly Dutch and French Huguenot populace, and that the mistrust in the opposite direction was mutual. That the winter storms were the worst in two decades and many a ship had been lost on the treacherous coast. That grand uncertainty reigned as to Britain and her war stance with France and Holland, or whether the troubles had quelled and the colony could be returned to its masters, Dutch East India Company.

Chikunda learned that his wife was now very pregnant, that she was being finely dressed and paraded about as the Bosun's concubine. And, in spite of this bragging, the commissions earned by Chikunda as the Bosun's assistant were keeping the local Dock Road whores in lucrative trade.

"We have three guilty verdicts." The Bosun was in an almost effervescent mood. "Hangings at last."

He acted as if fate had purposefully withheld his most beloved hobby for no good reason.

"It is of course a show for the townsfolk and those ships fortunate enough to be anchored in the lee of the hill. Let us remember this and make the best of it, by which I mean… make the show last."

It proved to be a terrible affair full of farcical pomp and macabre fanfare. The judges with black caps donned led the procession, a clergyman in tow reading ceaselessly from a black Bible.

No more than four-cornered pieces of black cloth tossed atop a white curled wig, they were still called "black caps", though they were not caps at all Chikunda was informed by the Bosun with hideous excitement, buoyant on the occasion.

The wind was up and the crowd was kept in peals of laughter as gusts played havoc with the grave air of stoicism that the craggy old judges, men wearing red cloaks and white neck scarves of a fashion, tried to maintain.

Drums and trumpets heralding the oncoming death wagon made slow progress up Strand street, so named as it bounded the beach or *strand* in the native Dutch.

The three condemned sat chained on hard boards heading west out of the town, over the Buitengraght.

The Buitengraght was the western-most boundary marked by the deep gutter channel that Chikunda recalled on his approach to the town that first night. It drained the valley pass between the mountains over to Baai van von Kamptz.

Along the rough path the wagon went, the mule walking solemnly through the heat. To the left was the signalling hill, to the right were small reed-covered dunes above a wharf with the ships at anchor beyond.

At the last tavern of the town, the procession halted and "One for the rope?" was called to the condemned.

They each drank a flagon of grog to steady their nerves.

Gallows Hill came into sight. It was a mound with the death apparatus atop.

"Vermaak, the old executioner wants me to use the new rapid drop," the Bosun was babbling to Chikunda as he limped alongside. "He is going soft in his old age. That's too quick. We'll give the audience their money's worth, eh?" He paused. "No wonder they need me to do the job properly!"

In the excitement of it all, the Bosun was a changeling. It was like he'd forgotten everything and was treating Chikunda like an old friend and comrade in arms, buoyant and full of vigour.

Two of the judges looking his way spoke earnestly and shook their heads, making their disgust plain.

But the bull-like man saw none of it.

The cart arrived at the gallows—a heavy cross beam with multiple rings set in a row along its lower face and supported on either side by columns of timber.

Gallows Hill was a chalky rise as high as a building's parapet roof. Its upper surface was paved with blue slate flagstones.

"Up you go," the Bosun ordered Chikunda, "make the ropes fast through those iron hoops."

Chikunda did his bidding, wondering how it had come to this in his passive life, playing assistant to an assistant murderer.

He had no option, was his answer. These were dead men regardless, and this obedience was merely play and pay to win his life back some day.

He climbed pegs set into a column to one side and then, seated with legs either side of the cross member, scooted out, fixing three ropes through the eyes and dropping their ends back down.

Jack the dog was there of course, lying a safe distance away in the shade, chin on his paws, watching.

Charges were read, repentance called for, heads bagged and struggling figures hoisted up as the cart creaked away with the ends of the ropes tied to it.

"A little too quick for my liking," the Bosun groused, "but neat for a first effort."

He slapped Chikunda on the back, his face dancing with a delight that Chikunda could scarcely believe he was capable of.

"You clean up here, dig the holes over there," he directed, pointing to a clearing in the small dunes where a domino pattern of recently disturbed grave-sized rectangles was in rows.

The crowd melted away and the Bosun sat with Vermaak the executioner on the hinged tail of the empty death wagon, sharing a murky green bottle of swigs and laughing with increasingly dark expressions.

Between shovels, Chikunda noticed a man with a shifty demeanour who had been hanging around the periphery of the crowd, gesturing surreptitiously to the Bosun from behind a tree.

Eventually, the Bosun saw the man and loudly announced that he needed a piss.

Behind the tree he went, and from his position, Chikunda detected the unmistakable haggling of a deal being struck.

The man bled away and walked on a trajectory so that the official executioner could not see him. The Bosun wandered over, club under his arm, farting impressively as he tied up his codpiece.

"Everything that leaves the body makes a man feel good, eh?" he said in English to the few lingering from the crowd to watch the burial. "No doubt the soul leaving gives equal ecstasy… if these black hearts had a soul," he declared, gesturing to the three corpses laid out in a row. "If so, we did them a tremendous service today. I'd prefer to keep them hanging there a few days as a reminder. But, we must follow the new rules I'm afraid."

The people moved aside from the bull-like man, and crossed themselves.

Out of earshot, he reached Chikunda and looked down into the pit being dug. It was waist deep.

"That's deep enough, he won't be here long," he instructed Chikunda. "Dig two more to the knee. You return tonight to dig them up for that man, and not a word of it. There's a bonus in it for you and a reduction of the debt your woman owes me. Now, I am coming to trust you. I will lead that drunken fool away, and when you are done, bring the wagon and equipment to the tavern." He turned to Vermaak. "Let's get out of this heat. My boy can finish up, I'll buy you a flagon."

As they walked, Chikunda heard the Bosun brag how his "boy had come to heal. He will do anything I tell him to do."

Chikunda sighed and seethed in silent agreement.

So long as his woman was in this man's grip, obedience was the only course. But, one way or another, Chikunda promised himself, the day would come....

By the time Chikunda arrived at the grog house and stood in the twilight outside, his master was raging drunk.

His only friend there was Vermaak, who had long since put the last of his conscious brain out of commission and was propped in a corner swaying gently to voices in his own head, oblivious to the Bosun's dark, incoherent rambling.

There was a wide moat of empty space around the pair, nobody paying them any attention beyond occasional disdainful or fearful looks.

It was already dark when the Bosun came through the door muttering about taking a piss when he saw Chikunda and his face lit up in a most extraordinary way.

"Ahhh! My boy is done!" He slapped Chikunda heartily on the back and bid him to wander with him as he stumbled toward a nearby tree to relieve himself.

The affair was unsettling.

The sudden change of character in the man, his camaraderie and friendliness—a fraud.

"I have been planning big things for you," he announced as his stream of urine hit the tree too high up and rebounded all over his breeches and boots. "You did me proud today," he enthused, "put on a fine show for which I gained much praise. This puts me in a mind to reduce the debt your woman owes to us. Was it eighteen strokes at last count?"

Chikunda felt the rancour rise in his throat.

Out here, in the dark, he could sling an arm about the man's throat and throttle him, interring him into one of those freshly dug graves without a soul noticing.

The urge to do so made his body go forward and retreat in a shudder of inner conflict and confusion.

"Boy?"

The word snapped him out of it.

"I asked you a question? Don't disappoint me now, just as I have become so pleased!" the ugly monster warned in a brittle tone.

"Forgive, sir," Chikunda heard his own voice speak, his mind still on murder. "It has been a day of fatigue."

"I was saying that I am pleased with you. You are proving to be a good asset." The wretched stench from the sewer that was the Bosun's mouth struck Chikunda in the face as the man shook off his business, speaking toe to toe. "Your woman owes us that debt. She will repay it on the fourth Sabbath day after she gives birth to your whelp… and I must add some strokes for the little black bastard that he'll be—proving that she has cuckolded me and my claim to it. But for now, I am offering a reduction from the eighteen we'd agreed on. I'm a kind man and you are a good worker. I offer it down to just ten. Now, isn't that fair?"

"It is," Chikunda answered, trying to keep the hatred out of his eyes. Dark as it was, he felt certain that the ferocity within would burn through the night and give the Bosun reason to rescind on this new and magnanimous offer.

"Good. Now. It is getting on in the hour and is about time that you went along to do my earlier bidding. I will take another drink. Beware not to be caught by the Watch in this matter, for I will swear no knowledge of it and you will be considered as breaking a curfew and a taboo, the sanction for which, I need not emphasize, is extreme. When you are done, you will bring me the bag of coins from the man who waits there. Understand?"

"Sir."

"Well, be off then," the Bosun staggered toward the alehouse's door where there was a crashing of heels and raucous laughter of a sea shanty struck out into the night.

With the full moon almost at its zenith, Chikunda found himself supporting the staggering weight of the solid blockhouse of the man down toward the strand street and on to his home and dungeon near the fort.

The bag of coins had felt weighty. With much glee and a promise of reward, the Bosun had pocketed it and been good as his word—a tankard of ale had been sent out to the street where Chikunda had waited under the stars for his master.

Unaccustomed to any alcohol, but motivated to swallow it on an empty stomach if only to wash the bitter taste of despair from his mouth and mind, Chikunda felt its buoyant effects immediately buckling his legs.

For the time that it lasted, the alcohol loaned to him a sense of relief from months of trial and tribulation.

"You have been a good boy today," the alcohol lubricated the Bosun's tongue. "And a further reward is in order. I was thinking that you may wish to see your woman?"

Chikunda felt like the man hat hit him with a shovel in the face. The words rang in his ears and he could scarcely believe it had been said.

"I would, sir," he spoke carefully so as not to upset this happy turn of events. "I would be very grateful, sir."

"I will arrange it," the Bosun assured and stumbled into Chikunda along his path.

Chikunda held him up and the man threw his full dead weight into that support.

Chikunda felt sick at the touch of this man, and wrestling with his vast solid bulk to keep him upright or pay the price for failing to do so played terror within him.

It felt as if a hog, stinking and smeared with the grime of an ugly life had reared up and was tottering down the road pushing itself onto him.

As they went, the Bosun spoke more, his voice warming, leaning against Chikunda ever more like an old friend, his tongue weaving scenes of wickedness and massacre scenes recalled from an embattled lifetime.

He spoke of how he and his family had been dreadful victims of fate and how he had sworn to make others pay the price for it.

"My father died of consumption before I was in my teens," he blathered. "Left my mother penniless and a drunken whore to sailors. I would hear them and hide my face from the shame of it.

Grunting and sighing until I wanted to vomit. One day I could take it no more and plunged a dagger into a man's back as he had my mother on her knees."

They stumbled on over the stagnating and stinking Buitengracht boundary gutter that sluiced the offal and blood of slaughtered animals, garbage and sewage from the town to the sea.

"I put to sea that very day. It was that or face the noose. And it was there that I truly learned the meaning of *suffer*. And for every moment I suffered, I returned the debt of it ten-fold. But now my life is here, in this place. I have a good job and fine prospects, and only one man between me and a very fulfilling life…"

He laid out his plans.

Murder!

Chikunda was drunk for the first time in his life, stumbling along a street trying to keep a man that owned him from falling. A man who had stolen his woman, had embroiled him in perpetrating tortures and the sale of executed corpses for use in unknown purposes.

And now this man proposed making him a mercenary to do his own private killing—the murder of his own boss.

"I already purchased the boat," the Bosun was explaining earnestly, as though the news of it heralded a great boon to both of their fortunes. "It lies at the fishmonger in Woodstock. You are to collect it and row back down the coast to the fort on the morrow. I have promised Vermaak that in your former life you were a man of the sea.

He will be my partner in this venture, you ken? Fifty-fifty… you understand what this means?"

Chikunda heard himself agreeing that he did.

"But of course, he's a tight-arsed Dutch bastard, he won't put up a penny for his partnership share. In lieu, he will regularly put to sea with you when needs be and pay for his partnership thus. It is really his silence that I am buying, and he knows it—hence the heavy price; his silence to allow me to work outside the service of the new overlords while we draw a salary from it. With the British garrison in the town, there is a demand for fresh fish, so you will go out on the sea daily, except for those happy occasions when there is work to do at the scaffold or whipping post. And, one of these days, not too distant, Vermaak—who cannot swim, you understand— will have an unfortunate accident. Of that I am sure."

Chikunda stumbled on in numb silence, Jack the hound, now with his ribs showing and his coat full of mange, shadowing them.

It was plain. He was to murder his boss' boss.

"Do you understand me, boy?" The Bosun was suddenly lucid of voice, the devilish plan he'd devised sobering him with excitement.

"Sir."

"That's a yes sir?"

"Aye, sir."

"You're a good boy. If you do this well—well, who knows? A kind master might forget all, or at least *most* of your debts, you understand? Indeed.

It may be time for you soon to have a little time with that woman of yours."

"I understand," Chikunda was suddenly very sober too.

Chapter 7

The Bosun's hangover proved to be an evil one.

Not a physical illness from alcohol.

No.

The man was far too pickled in the stuff over a lifetime to suffer that malaise. It was a different kind of hangover, a rebound in mood away from the glimmer of humanity that had soaked through his bitter personality. He seemed to be reeling from it.

In the mid-morning, the bolt on the door to Chikunda's dungeon clapped back for the first time, the door opened wordlessly and a plate of slop glued by the character of its own unfortunate contents to the chipped thing came clattering in.

The door slammed and bolted again.

It was done with a rapid caution, as if the insight doled out so freely to Chikunda the night before might escape to besmirch and even convict the master if he wasn't brusque.

For three days, Chikunda paid this price in silence and solitary confinement for seeing behind the monster's mask and hearing the master's plans.

On the fourth day, the door opened and stayed open.

When Chikunda did not emerge, "Lying sleeping all day, you lazy black bastard," the Bosun growled, unseen outdoors, in the gloom. "There's work to be done."

Chikunda appeared, blinking, into the sunlight.

"I have purchased a fishing vessel from the monger up at Woodstock beach," he said, as if mentioning it for the first time. "I require you to fetch it and get it beached at the bottom of Long Street before the cursed southeaster wind rises. You will use it daily when we have no other business to attend to."

"Thank you, sir." Chikunda scanned the courtyard as he always did, hoping to catch a glimpse of Faith.

Over the weeks, Chikunda fell into a routine, heading for the boat down at the shoreline below Strand Street—*De Waterkant*. It was pulled up at the beach between Long Street and *Heerengracht* Road, named for the ladies and gentlemen who strutted their finest on a Sunday.

Out through the small surf he'd pull the craft on heavy oars, Jack always his companion, wolfing down whatever offal Chikunda could find or spare for him of the bait.

He'd then follow the lead of the experienced fishermen, mostly slaves or freed slaves of Philippine and Malaysian extraction.

They were an excitable mob who talked loudly and lived wildly, but they had an uncanny instinct for what fish were about and where they could be found.

A variety of *snook*, cousins of the formidable barracuda would shoal, and then the strategy would always be for the boat that struck a shoal to holler *"VAS!"* as loudly as they could to the whole fleet that would pick up the cry and rapidly descend on the spot to frantically work dollies, shinned-up lead lures trailing a skirt of colourful leather tassels.

Over the side, would come flashing silver streaks of fish as long as Chikunda's leg, with snapping jaws of cobra-like teeth set like fangs at the front of their sleek pointed snouts.

On a good day, all on his own, Chikunda could almost sink his boat under the dead weight of these monsters from the deep.

On other days, he might almost sink his boat with spiny red lobster that almost nobody wanted to buy as they lived on carrion and drowned sailors.

Through tempests he went out and on days when the sea mist came down so thickly that he could barely see the transom of his boat as he leaned on the oars. When socked in by silver mist, the entire fleet would throw anchor, invisible to one another, and talk loudly until the blue sky returned once more.

Vermaak, the old executioner, rarely made an appearance, and it was always a welcome relief to Chikunda when he could get to sea before the inebriated old man staggered onto the beach.

If the old soak did make it, Jack would be clouted off the vessel and stand forlornly on the shore watching Chikunda pull the ruddy old man out to sea on powerful strokes.

On those rare occasions when Vermaak did make it, Chikunda always knew he'd be in for a tough day. The fleet of experts would abandon him and make their distaste for his cargo most obvious if he tried to join them.

On days like these, unable to follow the fleet, his pickings would be small and the Bosun would furiously make his usual threats with Faith's tender flesh as their focus.

Of the limited English that both Vermaak and Chikunda spoke, neither of them shared many actual words, so conversation while at sea was near-on impossible.

Time and again, Chikunda set the man up to go overboard and, unable to swim as he was, to the bottom.

A simple tug on the oars when the man was standing would send him reeling into the gunwale and cartwheeling into the water. But, try as he might, Chikunda could not murder the man in cold blood. Not even when the price for failing to do so was a mounting tally of licks by the sjambok on his wife's flesh.

Each time he arrived back with the man still aboard, the Bosun would remind him in graphic detail of how he would soon be stripping flesh from her back.

And yet, Chikunda could not do it.

The old rum-addled Vermaak would sit grilling and turning pink in the sun, muttering to himself and doing precious little fishing.

The upside was that each trip to sea would turn him off the whole enterprise for a week or more until those brain cells that might have remembered the unpleasant episode were killed off by rum, and he'd fold to the Bosun's urgings and try it out again.

With each passing day and with each ride that Vermaak made to sea, the Bosun became ever more furious and Chikunda's insistence that they were being watched by the fleet wore ever thinner.

Much as the pressure built for Chikunda to perform the simple task of seeing the man overboard, the picture of Vermaak's emaciated and already neglected delinquent son becoming an orphan would not let him do it.

And then, one day, as they got beyond the waves with the Bosun on the beach glaring a final warning at their departing, Vermaak turned and vomited copiously into their wake.

It was a scorching-hot day with an unpleasant dry wind coming off the distant mountains out of the northeast and the ocean was as flat as a lake.

Without looking at Chikunda, Vermaak circled his finger about, the universal signal to return to the beach.

"What's the problem?" The Bosun glowered as they surfed up the beach.

"I think he's ill, sir," Chikunda shrugged.

"Still drunk as a pig," the Bosun growled in Portuguese. "This was the perfect day for it, huh. Why did you turn about?"

"Not today," Vermaak gurgled in his poor English, on his knees. "I have eaten something bad."

"Eaten?" the Bosun repeated in Portuguese. "He stinks of cheap booze. Only got out of the whorehouse at sunrise, I heard. I've about had it with you," he rounded on Chikunda in Portuguese. "There would be no better day than today, and you turn back?!"

"I… I…"

"You? Nothing! That wife of yours…" the Bosun stammered in rage. "Every kindness I've shown you…"

His scowl was puce and a vein throbbed angrily as it snaked through his thinning hairline and across his forehead, amplifying the pox of wet festering skin rash that Chikunda had noticed over the months, slowly corroding the man's face,

"…Every forgiveness for your errors and insolence," he raged at Chikunda. "Every bit of decency and friendship, and you repay me, how? With a dereliction of…"

"Leave the man alone," the old executioner demanded in broken English, down on his knees, sliding beach sand with his hand over a new puddle hurled up. "I told the man to bring me back. Whatever you say to him in that monkey tongue of yours, you can do just as well in a common language, no? You make me wonder."

"I was only telling this fool that you were clearly not well from the outset, *Mijnheer*. He should never have taken you out, and now he's wasted precious time. I'll deal with him later." He turned to Chikunda. "Go on…" In English, he spoke, "Get…!"

As Chikunda heaved on the boat, a small wave lifted its stern, allowing it to be pulled back into the water.

The Bosun added, "And you better return with a full load, or don't come back at all."

As the two white men made their way from the shore, Jack spied his gap and darted forward, leaping into the boat.

Chikunda swung the bow into the shin-high white water, before giving the craft a shove and leaping in over the stern. A moment later he was on the rowing seat, leaning on the oars.

The small town slid slowly into the distance with each oar stroke.

Chatter among the fleet had been that no birds were working the ocean again.

This meant that the prized shoals of barracuda-like snook were absent. Everyone was loaded with traps and would be targeting lobster that were to be found in profusion off the kelp reefs southwest of the headland, beyond the wharf and Gallow's Hill.

Chikunda leaned on the heavy oars, wondering how long he could avoid the inevitable with Vermaak as the boat gurgled forward on a most peaceful ocean.

With the sun well up, he arrived at a small collection of boats where everyone seemed in a jovial mood with long-distance conversations echoing over the calm conditions with plenty of catch to be had.

The traps went over the side at regular intervals into the afternoon, full and creaking with red flapping life.

With not quite a half-load, the warm breeze that had steadily shifted to the north suddenly puffed its first icy gust. The change in direction brought with it a steady increase in strength.

By the time Chikunda tied off the excess retrieval rope of a crayfish trap just sent to the bottom, and had rowed to the next trap to empty it of contents and reset, the wind out of the north was driving wavelets and flecking fine spray.

Most of the fleet that had arrived earlier with a two-man crew to work faster, were already done for the day and had turned for home.

And you better return with a full load, or don't come back, kept echoing in his mind, the snarling face burned into his memory.

The fresh set of traps had just gone down and he needed to leave them a while, so he held station against the wind blowing him southward down the wild coast.

By the time the last heavy load came flapping life aboard, the wind was beginning to whistle.

He turned and pulled for home, standing against the oars and losing two yards of distance for every one that he gained.

As the sun inched across the sky, the only beach hospitable to a rowing boat in these deteriorating conditions, De Waterkant of the town, grew steadily more distant.

Picking up Gallows Hill in the close distance and watching it move in the wrong direction against the background of the signalling hill, he realized that the fight was lost. The wisest thing would be to cut his losses and run to save himself and save the boat.

To the south, that old lion's head of a mountain was wearing a thick mane of clouds.

Two days of storm would follow, the old cobbler had warned, and he'd confirmed these predictions several times since.

The northwest storm wind now had him fully in its grip.

He'd seen the lay of this coast on that first day up on the signalling hill. Ahead of the wind, in the direction it was blowing him, lay the awful black fangs of rock. They stood in military row out to sea all along the coast between him and the shoemaker's bay where he had first encamped.

There would be no safe port now, not until the angular black rocks gave way to the rounded white granite boulders to the south. Time was running out fast.

From the rowing seat, he looked over his shoulder and the bow, back toward the town and its very distant beach. It was clear that he'd crossed the threshold of possibility to make landfall there.

The time for hope was gone. Now was the time for action.

Chikunda shipped the oars and leapt up.

He invested precious moments dumping his catch back into the ocean—to buy freeboard for his boat from the wind-driven chop and make it easier to handle.

With a lighter boat, he was able to get out ahead of the wind, cutting a course across the wind and out to sea, making for the horizon to avoid the headlands of reef and rocks that stood between him and safety.

Inshore of him, angry surf was already beginning to burst over hidden reefs.

With the wind at his stern, the wooden boat of clinker design repeatedly yawed and broached with the speed he gained as he pulled steadily toward Schoenmaker's Gat bay.

Up above and beyond the signalling hill in the foreground, the distinctive wide profile of Table Mountain began to change as he ran fast along the coast, approaching the lion's head mountain from the sea.

The ridge he'd crossed on that first day when Jack had found him was now abeam of his starboard side.

This was the mark he was waiting for—and inshore he saw confirmation that the rocky shoreline was now all rounded white granite boulders.

In the far distance ahead, the four white beaches and the headland where he and Faith had camped for months until the shoemaker had found them was approaching fast.

Like welcoming arms, the headlands that defined the north and south boundaries of Schoenmaker's Gat bay welcomed him in.

A short time later, careful to avoid the offshore shoals where tall waves already thundered over angry water, he was quickly nestling into the protected southern corner of the bay where the ridge ran out to his old encampment.

This was known territory, and Chikunda felt relieved. Jack jumped out into the shallows and barked excitedly, recognizing the territory and his old haunt.

Chikunda dragged the boat high out of harm's way, tipped it over in the bushes and stowed the oars some distance away.

Then he considered his options.

It would be a hike up and over the *Kloof*, through the *Nek*, a pass in the mountain that divided Table Mountain from the lion's head mountain and down to the town to report himself and his boat as safe.

To fail to do so would only bring censure and sanction once more.

But the freedom of being away from the town and its oppressive overlords called to him like demons in the depths of his soul.

His urge was to run and keep running. To use what he'd learned about the land, about where authority had spread to, and about how to avoid all of that.

But there was Faith.

The promise from the Bosun that he may see her had never materialized.

His heart broke for her every time he allowed himself to imagine her face. She was in his every dream. As absent as she was, she remained ever present and the centre of his every decision.

She was over that hill and now not more than weeks from giving birth to his child.

But while he had this small freedom he wanted to celebrate it to the full.

His ankle had fully healed and he moved swiftly on long legs with an easy gait up and over the ridge, Jack running ahead then lagging as they went.

Over at von Kamptz's bay he could see the garrison hunkering down to ride out the storm.

He went down to enjoy a selfish moment, to a place where he'd found a fleeting and precarious peace with his wife some months before.

He drank again from the sweet water of the brook and sat a moment on the downy grass, listening to the frogs calling to their rain gods for a larger territory.

He looked into the cave on the beach where they'd slept and walked again on the mussel-shell infested beach, their brittle clinking sound when shattered under the heel of his boot yanking him through time to that moment when his delusion of safety had evaporated in a moment.

And what of the shoemaker now? he asked himself, regret crushing his heart.

The spectre of the man, Chikunda could see in the theatre of his own mind, coming down to forage as he had done a thousand times before in these very rock pools.

He was by now certainly returned to some savage retribution in his homeland, and Chikunda felt the weight of that guilt.

Had the man just ignored them, he would still be here, and they would be in precisely the position they were in—slaves to fate.

It was then that Chikunda had the urge to visit the old cave one more time.

"Come on, Jack."

He turned his back on this little encampment and quickly retraced those steps up the ridge and onto the contour path that would take him to the shoemaker's cave high above the site of the shipwrecked slaver.

It was as if nobody had been along that path and to the cave since Chikunda and the Redcoats had last left it.

Aside from unwashed containers ransacked by the wildlife and some debris blown about into the nearby bushes, everything still lay in the disarray he'd found it in, in the wake of the cobbler's departure.

There was nothing for him here but to visit old ghosts and bid his thanks to the departed man for sacrificing so much for so little gain.

He was about to leave when the fact that the cobbler would likely never return struck him, and that a treasure lay hidden.

Into the cave he went and through to the loftily named atrium.

Under the ledge, he felt the living thing he was seeking.

Out into the darkening drizzle he brought it and carefully unwrapped the length of it.

The two swords were pristine.

Chikunda felt the warrior spirit of long dead ancestors rising within him, wanting to see the glinting lengths of silver beauty once more.

With a snicker of sound and a gentle sigh the sword broke the embrace of its scabbard and slid a threatening hand's breadth open.

Unable to curb his curiosity, Chikunda gingerly drew his thumb across the cutting edge with the delicate touch of a butterfly. The deadly rasp of the metal seemed to whisper its sharpness and lethal capacity to slice in a way that no blade had ever done before.

The touch of it was almost mystical, and Chikunda checked his thumb pad to be sure that the skin was not peeled painlessly away at that light caress.

He closed it, but those ancestors deep within were curious beyond all rational thought, so he slid it open fully and gave the thing its freedom in the open air.

There was a curious balance to it, a life within that wanted to leap from his hand and twirl in a precise dance. It wanted to haunt the air with its droning sounds of menace.

This was truly a thing of great beauty.

It had a sway to its length and those handsome gun-blue undulations swimming all the way to its snub end. Even that truncated termination of the sword, where all other similar weapons he'd ever seen always came to a needle point, seemed somehow to boast of a pedigree in the art of killing more wicked than the sleekest fine point could.

Jack looked unsettled, wincing as he went from place to place, sniffing old familiar jetsam.

Chikunda felt eyes on him and shuddered. The eyes of his long-dead ancestors who had wanted to see the thing through his eyes, or the eyes of the shoemaker whose ghost might very well have returned to this small piece of paradise that he'd temporarily found and lost. Or perhaps it was the eyes of the sword's maker, for Sebastião had told him that when these swords left their scabbard, they always thirsted for blood before being returned.

It seemed a peculiar thought, but Chikunda felt an urge to pay a tribute to his trespass here and his mishandling of a possession that he did not own—albeit now only the legacy of an all but dead man's last worldly possession.

He took the sword and drew it gently over his forearm, watching fine hairs fall away and then his skin part open at the breath of its touch—white beneath the blackness until the blood washed the white away in a bright and stinging trickle.

With just the very gleaming edge having tasted a lick of him, Chikunda let his blood drip all about the camp in the manner that a witch doctor, a *sangoma*, would bleed a chicken to bless a home or *kraal*.

It was a ritual he made up as he went, but it felt as if it was a closure of a chapter and the paying of a debt.

"I am sorry for what we caused to you my friend."

Chikunda spoke aloud in Portuguese, his skin prickling in fear that an answer may emanate from some quarter.

"You are a man who stood tall above all other men for your humanity. May God be with you wherever you may be, shoemaker. May our paths one day cross so that I can recompense in whatever small measure I can for your sacrifice," he paused, "I trust that I may borrow these. One never knows when they might be useful, eh, cobbler?"

He echoed the man's words said to him in this very spot just months before.

High up the slope above, the wind droned in the trees and sheets of icy rain arrived in the lee of the mountain.

And then he left without turning back, the two swords wrapped in the length of canvass, the cobbler's dog quickly making haste to catch up.

He carried the weapons but knew not where to, nor why.

He knew not what he'd do with them when he got to wherever it was they were taking him.

Chapter 8

Approaching the Nek, the saddle between the mountains that divided the bays from the town, Chikunda was met by a haunting dirge of sound.

The day was almost over with angry bleak clouds making it almost twilight and phantoms of lower cloud, ethereal and fleeting, whipping through the gap.

The barrage of wind out of the north, funnelling through the pass, sung a cacophony of many voices.

As he crested, it was as if nature itself wished to hinder his return to captivity. At the skyline, the full force of the storm struck him in the chest with cannon blasts of air, each as heavy as a punch. The sleet it carried stung like icy shrapnel harvested deep in the South Atlantic.

Out in the bay, half a dozen bucking ships strained at anchor, dwarfed by the cobalt ocean beyond, facing into the tempest and rising swell.

Their masts and rigging were bare as witches' brooms and their crews battened out of sight.

In the fading light, he saw with horror how the pattern and distances between the ships were slowly changing.

Anchors were dragging.

He'd carefully stowed his load in a small crawlspace under a boulder off the path in the lee of the storm.

Empty handed, down the path he plunged toward the impending catastrophe.

As he ran, his mind bitterly protested.

What was he running for?

To assist people who enslaved him?

To avoid a sanction for not doing so?

To win approval?

There were no answers, just the blind urge to help another being in peril.

To his right, he could hear the roar of the river that ran into the Buitengracht channel.

Three thousand spine-jarring paces downhill and the track flattened out.

Jack was at a full gallop, enjoying the thrill of stretching his young legs with his new master giving chase.

It was now almost totally dark and he could see torches at the shoreline where the first of the boats was already in the surf line just off the town.

He reached a culvert where the Buitengracht water raged below, boulders tumbling down the channel sounding like giants plodding in the depths, the floor shuddering with each footfall.

Over it he vaulted at a sprint and on toward the cluster of torches.

Above the sounds of the ocean dumpers and the howling tempest, he could hear the crash of timbers and screams of drowning men.

In the dim light of the spluttering torches, the white of flung water and spray revealed a nightmarish scene—a ship in the wave line. It was tilted by the waves, careened over on its port side with its mast facing the beach and men clamouring and clinging to it.

Perhaps it was the howls of terror so fresh in his memory, the ones that still tormented his dreams at night, the screams of his own fated slave shipwreck that had delivered him to these shores; but some insanity drove Chikunda in his headlong dash. He didn't stop to think of consequences.

Driven by a manic instinct deep within, he threw his clothes aside as he ran and went out into the maelstrom, bounding naked on long legs like a gazelle over the incoming white water.

Shouts of surprise, horror and caution spontaneously rang out from the watching throng.

He grabbed the first body he came to and saw that it had no life still in it, so he skirmished with the rip of water on to the next.

He grabbed the thrashing unfortunate and the man raged to life in a blind panic. He tried to climb on top of Chikunda to get away from the haul of the sideways current in chest deep water.

Chikunda went with the man's force, under, the man clawing on top of him, using him as a step.

Born to a fishing tribe and accustomed to the ocean waves since he could toddle, Chikunda kept his head in the moment of panic. He did not fight but slipped out from under the man and let the current move him out of range before he surfaced a second later and a fathom's distance away.

The man was back down in the boil, swirling and tumbling.

Chikunda chose his moment and lunged in, grabbing the man from behind, sliding his arms under the man's armpits and locking his fingers behind the man's head. In part, to subdue the victim's attempts to fight and in part, to keep the man's head above water.

The ocean was drawing back for another mighty wave of white water and the suck of current made Chikunda's heels drag toward the horizon along the ocean's bottom as if he was ploughing a pair of long furrows out to sea.

On shore, Jack patrolled the water's edge in a panicked trot, bounding as if he had springs on his front legs to get a view of his master fighting the sea.

The next wave ended the slide, and hit them like a runaway bull, sending Chikunda and the victim tumbling head over heel back toward the shore.

This was the way of the ocean, and Chikunda knew how to beat it—relax and rest when the current carries you in a preferred direction, resist with minimum effort it's attempts to drag you away.

Three more cycles of drag out to sea and roll back in, and Chikunda had the man in thigh-deep water.

During the fight he had drifted half a cable in distance along the beach and away from the torches, but men were following them along the shoreline. They ran in when they dared and took the man from him.

Before hearing their thanks, Chikunda, naked, sprinted back toward the knot of the action, Jack keeping pace.

He bounded out once more to repeat his efforts.

When he had brought three men out, other saviours gained courage by his efforts and dared further into the surf trying to help, but they failed to strip their clothes off and Chikunda had to turn from his task to save his new assistants, their clothes sodden and acting like spinnakers, dragging them relentlessly into deep water.

"Take off! Take off!" Chikunda yelled in poor English at a man as he brought him, spluttering, to safety. "Water pull you!"

He pointed out to sea, pantomiming it for the watchers, not caring that he was naked and that women numbered among the panicked onlookers, seeing but not registering the ugly block that was the Bosun there under a hat running like a waterfall from its wide brim.

"OFF!" he emphasized, "DROWN!"

And he whirled, going out for a fourth man to save.

With a thunderous crash, the ship's hull was staved in by a gargantuan set of waves that rolled Chikunda up the beach to where the rapidly retreating spectators had just stood.

He stood there facing the ocean, alive with new thrashing bodies coughed out of the holds, his black nakedness glistening in the insipid light.

As the waves sent the last of half a dozen behemoth walls of water up the beach, Chikunda went in for his seventh victim and two naked white rescuers joined him, more tentative, up to their thighs only and less bold.

At the sight of the pair of naked white men, men ashore began herding the women together and steering them steadily away from the action.

When the ship's two halves had been decimated to threadbare planking and drifted far apart, the sea began to empty of life.

Some bodies still floated limply and were washed ashore, but none fought for life.

Chikunda crawled, naked, as high as he could above the highwater mark and collapsed in exhaustion there, his clothing long since washed away. Jack desperately tried to lick his face as if re-establishing a connection in peril.

The town physician was down attending to the survivors, the priest attending to the dead.

Nobody paid attention to Chikunda until the Bosun swayed over, Jack getting up and clearing out of striking distance.

"So, you disappear with my boat, and then reappear, naked out of the night, you black bastard? Then you show pretence at being the hero?" he accused in Portuguese. "Pick yourself up, hide that shameful nakedness, and get back to your cage. I'll deal with you later."

He turned and wandered nonchalantly off with his hands still behind his back and Jack slunk back.

Chikunda rolled to his knees, groaning for his abused body and spluttering out the swallowed water.

All about was the flotsam of the wreck, sodden and covered in the muck of yellow foam whipped up like egg whites by the fury of the surf.

Unnoticed in the near dark, he stumbled about, looking for fabric enough to cover his nakedness, and then he started for his prison.

The Bosun arrived horrendously drunk much later.

A thud and Jack's yelp beyond the bars announced his stumbling approach.

Chikunda heard the dog's nails clatter away on the cobble street as he scurried to escape.

"Y'a black bastard," the man slurred at the grating to the cellar. "Took my boat and gone, eh? And where to? I'd thrash the hide off you but for the governor's wife."

He paused so long that Chikunda thought he'd imagined it or the man had stolen away, but then he spoke again.

"That filly has an eye for a black cock too, I might tell you. Took an unhealthy interest in you, all naked frolicking in the surf like you did. Now the governor wants to see me, and you know what happens if it's not good, eh?"

Then the door bolt shot home, locked from the outside and the Bosun blundered away muttering darkly to himself.

Chikunda lay in the pitch and silence of the dungeon, the rain still clattering onto stone outside.

Moments later came the crash of the man going through the front door.

Time stretched as Chikunda's mind raced to all the possibilities of what might happen.

A few moments later, there was another crash on the floorboards above and Faith screamed.

Chapter 9

They trudged in silence up the path that ran alongside the Buitengracht channel, still a torrent draining two days' worth of deluge from up in the mountains.

"Walk," the Bosun would periodically order Chikunda. From his hand swung the heavy wooden club.

Try as he might, Chikunda could not read his master's mood today.

Two days after the storm, and two days before this hike, he'd gone to the fort looking sullen. As he'd left he'd locked Chikunda in the basement and threatened unholy cruelties if his visit met bad tidings.

In the late hours of that night, with the full moon casting sharp vertical shadows from a clear and still sky, the gargoyle that was the Bosun's face had smeared itself against the dungeon's bars, growling inarticulate nonsense through the window grate.

It was guttural and full of references to bodily functions and dimensions.

Quite out of character, he hadn't even tried to kick Jack.

Among the garble, had been good tidings from the Governor and many accolades for the happy master for owning such a prize beast.

Now, as they trudged on up the Nek in silence, Jack slunk a few paces behind.

They were heading for the abandoned rowing boat in the shoemaker's bay.

When they reached the dinghy, the Bosun would never allow the dog aboard, so Chikunda rounded on him.

"Get! T'sak!" he hissed at the dog, making a start toward him to chase Jack back down to the town.

"Leave the dumb cur," the Bosun ordered. "Let it walk over the hill with us. Make a pitiful meal for a leopard on the return, but still…."

And that? Chikunda wondered. The Bosun had wished an unpleasant fate on the dog, but in the tone of an old friend.

It was confusing.

Chikunda's mind set to unravelling what might be up with this irrational swerve in character and demeanour.

The man was still mostly drunk, and that could be an answer.

As they trudged in silence through the dewy morning air, ever up toward the cliffs and clouds and the pass between them, "*Allaaaaahhhhhhhuuu Ak-bar…*" a *muezzin* crier in the Moslem minaret struck a ululating tune.

"*Allaaahhhhhhuuu Ak-bar…*"

The sound of it was crisp and clipped on the morning air, ringing out melodiously from the Bo-Kaap community to their right, overlooking the town.

"*Allaaahhhhhuuu Ak-bar… Allaaahhhhhuuu Ak-bar… Ashhadu an la ilaha illa Allah.*"

It sent Chikunda's mind racing back to the drunken, slurring arrival of the Bosun, back from his summoned visit to the fort and drunken binge into the small hours.

"Allaaahhhonnngblack-cock…" the Bosun had yodeled in English, coming up the cobbled lane two drunken nights ago.

"Allahhhong-llllllong-llllonnngblack-cock…."

He'd lampooned the daily call to prayer that spiced the air over the town with its echo of Malaysian heritage.

"Your thick cock did the trick, boy!" He'd started yelling publicly to Chikunda when he was close enough, crashing headlong into the bars of the cellar window.

This had made him roar with laughter and he'd pealed once more into another throaty rendition of self-amused wailing. "Allahhongblack-cock… Allahhhonnng-llllllong-llllonnnngblack-cock".

"Shut up, you drunken sod!" someone had boomed from one of the neighbouring houses, sending the Bosun into a staggering, club wielding rampage in the direction of the complaint, his threats of official privilege hurled in response toward the unseen complainant.

"That thick black cock did it boy!" He'd come staggering back to the barred cellar dungeon and roared his gormless newfound wisdom to the still night air.

He'd repeated it with unbridled hilarity until it became a gut-wrenching cough.

The laughter had ended in a heavy glob of phlegm spat onto the cobbles, the sound of its wetness slapping the ground echoing like a clicked finger down the cobbled street.

"Y'a get some sleep y'a fine stallion," he'd eventually roared and then crashed through the door of the house above.

Chikunda had lain for another sleepless night under the creaking boards of the woman he loved, the wife he'd die for and the child he would soon hear.

From the day of his surrender, he had not yet been allowed so much as a glimpse of or word to Faith. Always locked in the house, he'd only seen her shadow within, heard her voice seldom and her cry often.

The next day, the Bosun had suffered the usual hangover in attitude.

Another hangover of self-loathing and silence.

And on the second day, Chikunda had been let out of his pen and sent on errands.

In the town, eyes had been on him from every quarter, words spoken behind hands, but a nod here and a smile there suggested that his standing had risen immeasurably in the small town.

This morning he'd been fetched early and told, "We walk to fetch the boat. I'm coming with to ensure my fine stallion comes to no harm, valuable as he now is."

Valuable as he now is.... The words kept echoing in Chikunda's head, his mind trying to discern what he could from the intonation of it. It was at once encouraging and daunting, and the Bosun seemed to be squeezing every last torture he could from the obscurity and what he wasn't saying.

"And that woman," he now dropped offhandedly. "Not as valuable, but still useful... and of course problematic."

That was all he said; Chikunda's eyes on him begging for more but daring not to voice it.

As they went, Chikunda smelled the stale smell of excessive alcohol processed into sweat, and he saw a stagger in the Bosun's walk, the damp crescents of wetness staining at the man's armpits.

Strangers they passed kept a wide berth and found reasons to face the other way and not greet them.

The Bosun moved cautiously, his eyes bloodshot red and not focusing properly, his nose like a glowing coal on his face.

Eventually, the water of the stream ran clear and fresh down past them as they got above the settlement, well up the Nek from the Buitengraght.

The Bosun stopped to drink with a cupped hand and Chikunda took time to peer down toward the beach where he must shortly navigate the dinghy in through the still-large swells wrapping in there.

Jack was there, of course, his tongue hanging out and panting ten paces behind, patiently waiting for his turn at the brook.

The two halves of the wreck from days before were some distance apart. A little army of scavengers attended each of these, the hulks being deconstructed for their timers, the minor valuables long since secured at the fort.

He could pick out the house where Faith was locked at this very instant. It was two streets up from the stone fort and three streets in the direction of the signalling hill. It ran up to the Square, to the *Plein* in the local Dutch dialect, named after the settlement's founder, van Riebeeck.

Chikunda heard the stream water running past change its tune—it had gained a tinkle. Impulsively, he turned from the view and looked directly at the boiling and beer-frothing bubbles from the new feed.

"Just topping it up," the Bosun explained with a laugh.

The stumpy thing in his hand had an open sore on it. It was out through his breeches and arcing a stream of urine—so yellow it looked like it may employ a doctor—into the river that made a brief stop in the town's reservoir before its overflow flushed into the Buitengracht.

"Let them all taste what fine grog I swallowed, eh?"

He shook the thing vigorously and it disappeared into his codpiece.

"Let me explain," he began, in an ominously friendly tone as they continued their walk. "You have now gained a significant ally in the wife of the Governor. She harbours a quaint notion that those useless wretches you so boldly hauled from the sea were worth our time. Worth the risk of my valuable property. An English convict ship full of inmates you saved, no less. On their way to Australia. You know what a convict is?"

"Sir… yes. A prisoner."

"Indeed. White, but no better than you, a slave. So hardly worth the heroics, no? But, that said, it seems the act impressed, even if the action was questionable."

"Sir?"

"Not very bright, are you? No matter." He sighed theatrically, as if talking to an imbecile. "People thought you were very brave, and a fine specimen at that. The Governor's wife most particularly. Unsurprising, I'd say. An old man like that… his quill no doubt long since out of ink, eh? Now there's something for you to think about when you lay in your dungeon at night rubbing dubbin into the old leather."

And he laughed again, twirling his club round and round.

Jack, back in tow, halted nervously.

"Well, let's just say, the price I was offered for you could set me up very nicely back home." He paused, examining the thought as the crest of the mountain's saddle came into view. "Then again, I'm not sure I want to leave this place anymore. My life is good here. The bay is handsome, the women compliant at the right price, and when you finally grow some and see to it Vermaak takes a swim—well... This business becomes my stage."

He stopped and mopped his brow, running as it was with rivers of sweat, his shirt drenched through and the smell of alcohol on it rank.

He surveyed Table Bay beyond the town, grunted and turned to begin the descent toward Schoenmaaker's Bay and the dinghy beached there.

"I'm getting used to this place and tired of the sea. I'll be the boss then, the boss of all discipline in the colony. The plan is all worked out, you see... and there is something in it for you too. I've grown to like you. Even respect you, respect you as much as a man of breeding can respect, you know..."

He waved absently toward Chikunda as if he didn't wish to insult him by voicing his thoughts.

"With Vermaak gone, I can do things my way. With age I've come to understand myself."

With the ascent behind him, he was gaining strength, slapping the club into his palm as if he were acting out the dream that ran behind his eyes, glazed and euphoric in the laying out of a bright future.

"I'm an artist. I've found how a man lives, and how he dies, and where the line is between them. It is a secret of my trade that I will share with you. Who knows… times are changing fast. There may come a day when I'll set you free—that's if I decide not to sell you now. And right now, I must admit… it is appealing."

It was at this instant that Chikunda realized the man was insane and possessed by the devils that came from the whores. The devils that had steadily been ravaging the Bosun's appearance—corroding his skin, pocking it with infection and worsening his mood with the corruption likely rotting his bones.

The realization had scared Chikunda in a way he had never been scared in his life before. Not scared of the physical man, but afraid for his own soul, his own Christian soul. The Bosun had halted, his eyes glazed, envisioning his new life and galloping ambitions. Then he began to amble again, down the path as it wound in the cool shade of the mid-morning through the glen with the blue of the Atlantic twinkling through trees.

It was as if he was possessed by another soul, one with no knowledge of the cruelties he'd so vigorously visited upon Chikunda from the outset and until this day. Or at least, until he was blind drunk.

"My finances, I confess, well, they're not the best. Your friends, the two hundred we salvaged from the holds of the slaver and sold? They fetched a fair price. The Captain, bless him, was a man of honour who met the debts to the crew. They used their wage to sail on out within the month. Me? I rented the house from a widow. Paid up front for the half year. Enjoyed myself at the tavern and beyond, and why not, eh? But time is running out. There's the rent to pay again. Our fine work as assistants in keeping order produces good drinking money. And there's the thing I've been impressing upon you, to get on with it. The promotion with Vermaak out of the way will— well, I'll live comfortably."

He put his hand on Chikunda's shoulder and a shudder went through Chikunda. His urge was to pull away in horror, but bravery is in overcoming fear, not the absence of it and prudence is the better part of valour. These had been his mother's teachings to him from his first memory of her, so he kept his pace and route unchanged.

He walked with that hand on his shoulder, his skin crawling.

It had the heftiness and chill of a viper lying there.

"My language, the one you speak, Portuguese. It has its roots somewhere, you know." The Bosun went on a tangent. "It came from a city called Rome. That city once ran an empire. Now, the rulers of that empire had the *right* idea. They allowed artists like me to clean up the place by putting on vast theatre for the population. And that is what I intend here, once I have my way. More than that, I have calculated a commission for my work and a schedule for how we shall be paid. An ordinary whipping, and we'll get paid one fee. Strangulation, another fee. My top fee earner will be breaking on the wheel."

And he looked positively ghoulish, clearly enjoying Chikunda's alarm at the details.

"It's doubtful you've had the pleasure of knowing what that is, but I'm a master at it. We fix our prisoner to a wheel. Well, to be sure, it is more of a cross than a wheel, but you get the idea. And then begin with a hammer out at the extremities, breaking the bones as we reach the body. I'll leave you to think it through."

They came to a switchback in the path. Chikunda remembered it from his ascent after beaching the boat. Below them, he could see the path returning in their direction and then another switchback to make it an 'S', turning away again back toward the sea and a final descent on to the beach.

"Centuries ago, in my land, we had a purge of witches. Most people don't appreciate the truth of what drove that effort. Yes. Some women were possessed and the priests were right to convict them, but an entire economy arose around it. You see, as you know and agree, I am an artist in these matters of torture and death. But I am also a learned man."

His insanity was now clear for Chikunda to see. His voice a note higher in octave, his excitement palpable.

"I have the gift of reading, and I have made it my business to study these matters. Let me explain to you the economics of the witch trials and the kind of commissions I borrow from them, and intend to propose to the Governor. I share this with you because you are becoming my partner in this."

He cleared his throat as if to deliver a sermon.

"Let me tell you this history and teach you the business. In 1765, around the time I was born, the celebrated jurist, William Blackstone, in his Commentaries on the Laws of England—a country that influences all Europe—asserted, 'To deny the possibility, nay, actual existence of witchcraft and sorcery is at once flatly to contradict the revealed word of God in various passages of both the Old and New Testament.'"

He looked at Chikunda with the madness raging in his eyes and Chikunda felt the urge required of him to nod agreement.

"Good. Now, that harks to the original promulgated by Pope Innocent the Eighth who, in fourteen eighty-four, appointed Messieurs Kramer and Sprenger to write a comprehensive analysis, using the full academic armoury available to them."

The more he recited this grisly citation, the more the excitement of it seemed to sober his earlier ill appearance.

"With exhaustive citations of scripture and of ancient and modern scholars, they produced the *Malleus Maleficarum*, the *Hammer of Witches*. This will mean little to you, but it is aptly described as a most terrifying document. What it comes down to, you see, is that if you're *accused* of witchcraft, you're a witch. Torture is the unfailing means, especially vigorously applied, to demonstrate the validity of the accusation. Under that just law, there are no rights for the defendant, of course. There is no opportunity to confront the accusers. Little attention is given to the possibility that the accusations might be made for impious purposes such as jealousy, revenge, or the greed of the inquisitors. Because—and this is the cornerstone of my proposal and why I am explaining to you how I will become wealthy—the best part of the law is that the inquisitor is given the *right* to confiscate for his own private use and benefit, the property of the accused. Do you understand? If I get this proposal right, I will be able to confiscate the property of anyone I can convict of a crime."

Chikunda nodded dumbly. This ancient church law was a vision of hell that he had never been taught in the Mission. It's proposal now, even in a brutal town, seemed insane.

"This manual, the *Malleus*, taught me all I know about punishment. It was designed to release demons from the victim's body before the process kills her. Of course, that may be the case, I don't know, but it is a crowd pleaser that recalls the greatness of Rome in Europe."

The Bosun put his hand again on Chikunda's shoulder and a fresh bolt of horror racked his whole body, down to the soles of his feet.

"The truth is, it became an expense account fraud. You see, all costs of investigation, of trial, and indeed of execution were borne by the accused or her relatives, down to the private detectives hired to spy on her, wine for her guards, banquets for her judges, the travel expenses of a messenger sent to fetch a more experienced torturer from another city, and the faggots, tar, and hangman's rope. Sounds good, no? Some will need adaptation in this gentler age, but you get the idea."

A word left Chikunda's mouth, but he didn't know what it said, his mind was numb.

"This is where my plan can work, a bonus to the members of the tribunal for each prisoner we deal with. We get paid, and I make a donation back to the accusers and judges friendly to the idea. And here is why it will work: The more who, under torture, confess to their heinous sins, the harder it becomes to maintain that the whole business is *not* necessary, you follow? Since each accused will be persuaded to implicate others, the numbers grow out of hand. This is the benefit of being an educated man like me. To devise a beautiful plan for doing business by mere adaptation of what was already laid out for us all those centuries past."

They were beyond the switchback and on the final descent.

"How shall we increase our work? Where shall we find ever more condemned to be sent to our tender mercies? Well, what about the ship and its survivors that you so valiantly saved? There are many plying these waters, making their way from dear England around this coast to Australia. I suggest we offer them an alternative here, in this colony, allowing the ship to return in half the time to replenish its load. Then there is the Bushmen question that ought to be seen to, with a decisive hand. A whole continent full of kaffirs like you, slow to learn and quick to anger. The prices for our attentions would be lower, but that is no matter—our costs are already fixed, eh? And your arm does not easily tire."

Waves of nausea were washing through Chikunda at what this madman was proposing and intending to embroil him in.

It was as if Jack understood, as well. He traipsed further behind, his head and tail hanging low, scowling a lament.

But the Bosun was so lost in the fantasy world he was describing that he failed to notice anything else.

"You can see why I need a stout fellow like you," he said to Chikunda in most flattering terms. "The work will be long and drawn out, but very satisfying and lucrative."

And they walked on in silence, thoughts reverberating within Chikunda's mind as if they were themselves devils looking for a place to take their root.

"But then there is the question of the woman."

Those words were like a cold hard slap in the face to Chikunda.

"Were I to abandon this dream, sell you and purchase a new life back home, I'd of course take her, as she'd be quite a novelty where I come from."

He was speaking absently, asking the question of himself aloud, as if Chikunda wasn't there. Contemplating it as he would an option to transport any ordinary head of livestock or divest of it in a more profitable way.

"But we both know what the newborn will look like, don't we?" he addressed Chikunda directly. "A little frizzy head and nowhere near my skin tone. And that's not the kind of truth I want following me. Though with your fine physique, I could cultivate the child for a few years and then get a decent price but I'm not sure that the investment would be worth the profit."

Chikunda's vision started to waver. He'd never experienced a sensation like it. There was a flapping in his ears like a vast flock of birds was taking off about him. His view ahead began to close in from his periphery, night time coming from the edges. Only a tunnel of light stretched directly before him, wobbling fast back and forth, as if the scene was coming toward him and receding all in the same instant.

The Bosun's voice seemed to hum, slowing and slurring. There was a feeling of faintness washing through Chikunda's body, sweat prickling all over.

"...so the buyer from Swellendam," the Bosun was chatting cheerily, "will collect her within a fortnight, and..."

"What?" Chikunda found that he had halted, and was looking down at the Bosun who stopped also but did not turn his face towards him, only cocking his eye to look up at the tall black man as if surprised he could talk.

"What?" Chikunda heard himself ask again, his fists beginning to ball.

"The deal is concluded, you see. No more friction then between us."

The sound was like lightning coming out of the sky and shattering his eardrums. In its wake, the Bosun had hit the ground with his spine first and Chikunda was over him, ready to deliver another blow, but something made him hold it back. He allowed the Bosun to sit up. The man came up on one hand, the fingertips of his other examining the void in his mouth where three teeth had been only moments before. And then he wiped his mouth with the back of that hand and examined the smear of blood, pouring as it was from the roots vacant roots of teeth ripped out by the blow.

"You will die for this, boy," he said low and growling. "I will kill you slowly!" It built to a roar from that barrel chest.

Chikunda hit him again, now out of self-defence, to keep him down.

He rolled over and over and came up fast—much faster than Chikunda had imagined this man could move. He came swarming in, swinging the heavy club, aiming for Chikunda's hands, his elbows and knees. It was as if he had been trained in the same stick fighting that Chikunda was an expert in. He understood to ignore the natural head shot that came as instinct to any man and rather go for the vulnerable joints and limbs.

Chikunda was like a panther, leaping aside, making him miss and desperately looking for a weapon to protect himself.

A fallen branch was five paces away. As he grabbed it, the Bosun was on him, landing a glancing blow off his thigh with the club. He rode it and took most of the sting out of the blow.

"You're a dead man," the Bosun was saying over and over again, his eyes demented and red froth boiling out of his mouth from the exertions of the attack.

Chikunda parried the next club blow with an overhand sweep of the branch and reversed the thrust, coming up and under the Bosun's over-extension in that miss. He hit him across that ugly, red, swollen drinker's nose and a fine mist of blood puffed out in an arc.

The rotten branch snapped, one half spinning into the distance.

Chikunda dropped the stump he was holding and fled.

"You're a dead man!" The Bosun's eyes seemed to be swivelling in his head, the force of the blow making him stagger.

Jack was in a frenzy, the scruff of his neck bristling with hair, his barking an insistent clamour.

The Bosun swung the club at the dog and he ran away with his hind legs overtaking his front but turned and came nipping back in.

"No, Jack… get away!" Chikunda was yelling.

And then from his breeches and under his shirt, the Bosun produced a dagger, its blade proportions the size and shape of a flat hand, black and lethal.

"I'm going to cut your balls off, boy. I'm going to make you eat them, and then I'm going to feed that big black cock to your whore."

Chikunda turned and ran.

He ran for his life, Jack with him as if it were a sudden game.

"I'm going to get you!" the thing was roaring from behind. "And when I get you, I will do it slowly…. I'm right behind you, look behind you!"

Chikunda could hear that the man was losing ground, Jack going back to snarling and then racing to catch up again. Chikunda needed the demon to lose ground. He needed as much distance as he could get to survive this.

He was off the path and bushwhacking, heading for a prominent granite outcrop.

Behind him he heard the Bosun fall, going down heavily, but he did not look back.

When the Bosun's threats resumed, he sounded out of breath and quite distant.

Chikunda dived into the rocky formation, hitting the granite boulder a glancing blow with his head that had him seeing a private light show. He slid in on his knees under an overhang.

There, he fought mightily, ripping out small piled rocks with his bare hands, the white of his skinned flesh showing where the black of his skin was ripped away by the frantic efforts to dig.

The sound of the Bosun's voice was closing fast now, his ragged breathing audible in his shouts.

The bundle came out of the hole at that instant.

Chikunda felt the distinctive handle grip.

He grabbed the corner of the fabric and the contents spun, the wrapping unpeeling.

Out fell the swords just as Jack's barking announced the Bosun.

With a *whooooosh*, the silver length of the katana flashed in the sunlight as the Bosun came barrelling in, his club high and ready to crush Chikunda's skull.

The blade flew and caught the club at its midpoint.

Chikunda barely felt the impact as the blade went through it in one sweep.

Staggered by the sudden turn of advantage, the Bosun stared at the stump of club he was still holding and then stared at the sword.

"You have one choice left in your miserable life, but you don't have the balls for it, boy."

Chapter 10

Chikunda reached the boat and laid the Bosun down gently beside it.

Jack was trotting gaily alongside now, his mood entirely lifted.

Chikunda looked about.

It was deserted. Beach sand as white as salt and just as fine stretched to the shoreline under a crisp blue sky. Not a single track of footfalls betrayed any hint of visitor to this magnificent bay.

He sat down heavily onto the upturned boat, pulled up as it was beyond the white sand and laid in the hardy bush where the dirt began. He surveyed again with surreal disbelief the handiwork of that sword.

With his club severed through by a single blow, the Bosun had challenged Chikunda with not having the nerve to do it.

He'd goaded him, saying how he'd fucked his wife and this slave-minded man had done nothing.

Cornered and with terror obliterating his mind, Chikunda felt welded to the spot. He wanted only to be away, and, yes, he was terrified of this man and the consequences that would already be coming for what he had done.

He'd waved the sword in a crisscross before him, pushing the Bosun backward in an unconvincing mock attack.

The Bosun had moved but laughed at it.

Chikunda had then been out of the rocky outcrop that had cornered him. He'd turned and backed up to get around the outcrop and perhaps dash away again. The Bosun had followed into the gap his retreat had created.

Again, he'd swirled the sword but the Bosun had stood his ground.

"I want to go, sir. That's all I want. I want my wife and to leave this place. We have served you well, but it is time. I am sorry I hit you, I don't know why it happened, but all I want is to be gone."

He'd heard himself pleading. He'd not planned any of it, not thought any of it through. He'd been reduced to pure animal desire for freedom and retreat in the face of circumstance.

"And just look at you, boy," the Bosun had sneered, confident he had the dominant mind. "You're no master, so you deserve to be a slave. Put that thing aside and we'll see."

He'd emphasized it by stepping into range.

Years of stick-fighting instinct fuelled by adrenaline sent the sword crossing between them, establishing the boundary in a blur.

In that instant, the Bosun had raised his arm up and that formidable snub tip of the sword had opened his forearm with just a whisper of sound. The wound had yawned wide open, a gush of blood spurting from it instantly.

The insolence of it had driven the Bosun over the edge. He'd checked his arm and then hadn't checked his anger, lunging across the space.

Chikunda had fallen back a pace and parried to the side, the sword drawing a *whoosh* through the air in the shape of a rainbow's arch.

With almost no impact from the carnage reporting through the katana's handle, Chikunda had watched in horror as the Bosun fell, twitching and spurting, nearly cleaved in two, sliced diagonally from neck to sternum.

The ugly man had lay there gurgling, his eyes clouded in shock, his mouth working in soundless outrage.

A final macabre death dance ran through him and then there was only the breeze through the trees and the blood soaking into the thirsty earth.

Chikunda had stood back in shock at what he'd done.

In the rage and anguish, he'd reacted with little force as he could, but no court of a white man would believe it.

This would be the end of the road. Before the sunset on this day, the course of his life or his death would be fixed.

To run?

To surrender?

And what of Faith?

What of Faith?

If he ran, she would be lost to him forever. His unborn child in slavery forever.

If he handed himself in, they'd be lost to him forever, because this was murder.

Chikunda had known too well how these people's justice worked; he had helped execute plenty of men who had been guilty of far less than killing.

Could he spirit Faith away?

Could he bury this man and feign ignorance? Claim he had gone alone to fetch the rowing boat?

The site of all that blood was well off the path, nobody would find it.

But then, more than a few townsfolk had seen them walking up the hill together... and who else had this man told of their trudge to recover the boat?

Again, he'd looked down in disbelief at the scene around his feet.

He could clean this site, he could put the body in the boat and...

And, what? he'd asked himself.

Row it to the town, was the answer that had kept echoing in his mind. Let God's will be done. "God's will be done on earth as it is in heaven." He'd spoken the words of the Lord's Prayer.

Now on the beach and covered in the man's blood, Chikunda sat there looking at the state of the waves, still running large after the storm that had recently come through.

There were lulls between the sets and gaps enough between the waves to safely put to sea and begin the grim task of rowing to the fort.

He looked at the dead man at his feet. The Bosun had started to stiffen with *rigor mortis*, his pallor sallow. Even his red, pitted, alcohol-destroyed nose had faded ashen in death.

Chikunda started to cry.

Jack got up from where he'd been lying, perpetually guarding the perimeter as though he understood the gravity of the situation.

Chikunda cried for his wife, soon probably a widow. Jack nuzzled in next to him and he put his arm around the dog and cried into its coat.

He sobbed for his unborn child, coming into a world such as this.

And then he collapsed into lamentations for the dream that was shattered so many times. The dream he'd so often been forced to diminish, and then devalue in the cold reality of life going indifferently by—in the crosshairs of others whose ambitions traded in the currency of stranger's lives.

He looked at the upturned boat and saw in its place a canoe, the schoolroom of his childhood. His eyes swept over the brilliant white sand to the azure blue of the sea, and he saw it not as what it was now, but as the memory of laughter and family and abundance.

He closed his eyes and the image did not fade, the touch of the dog leaning against him evaporated from his reality.

Palm trees as far as the eye could see down the coast, the crash of waves and wash of the shore morphed into laughter, and Chikunda began to laugh. In his laughter, he became too terrified to open his eyes to what he knew he would see before him, for what he knew he must now face.

And the laughter became mania, and the mania tumbled to tears once more.

It was at this instant, in the dark behind his lids, in the echo of his own crazed howling that he asked himself if the spirit of madness had leapt out of this dead thing at his feet and into him.

The thought of it sobered Chikunda and he opened his eyes again.

In the madness of these moments with his life collapsing to new lows, he sunk into a fetal position next to the dead man. He looked into those slit eyes still open and lifeless, the mouth yawning wide with rotten teeth. It was a vision of terror, and Chikunda turned away, got to his knees, stood and walked. He ascended the path onto the ridge and followed it until he came to the great granite rock at its end.

Jack trotted next to him, keeping vigil for any threat.

They climbed onto the granite prominence at the ridge's end and below them was the shell beach and the spring of sweet water.

He went down, past the cave he'd inhabited with Faith for two moons and on to the sacred rock in the shape of a praying nun that had kept them safe.

Before it, he fell to his knees and began to pray.

Chikunda lost track of how long he had stayed there, but when he stood, the blood from the carcass that had covered him was stiff and cracking.

God had answered him and he knew what he must do.

It was to allow fate to take its course, and for him to be a man and face whatever was due and coming.

Without another thought and with no more fear, he stood and walked away.

The rhythmic plop of the oars and sigh of the boat slipping over the ocean was the most comforting sound Chikunda had ever heard.

Jack would not be coaxed aboard. He would not be trapped in such close confines to the corpse of the Bosun.

Looking out over the stern as he went, he watched Jack become a lonely dot on the snow-white beach. And as he watched, Jack turned and began to trot toward the path over the saddle of the mountain, as if he understood.

The vast mountain range running south seemed suddenly to Chikunda to be men standing shoulder to shoulder facing his direction out over the Atlantic, the peaks as their heads.

He felt an urge to count them and came to a dozen.

Twelve.

He counted them again.

Twelve? he thought, *twelve like the Apostles!*

The coincidence of it struck him.

Before the very alter of the praying nun and under the bowed heads of twelve mountainous apostles, God had spoken to him and he could only obey.

It was without fear then that he pulled on those oars, a fathom of travel at a time, closer and closer to the destiny that delivering the butchered Bosun would bring.

Seals languishing in siesta on the surface raised their heads as he passed, a whale courted death blowing its plume just a league out to sea, and a pod of dolphins turned from their busy southerly migration heading in the opposite direction to cruise under and alongside his dinghy until they satisfied themselves that it was of no interest, and went clicking and squeaking away.

Gallows Hill came ominously into view.

He passed the few stragglers of the fishing fleet still out in the fading afternoon, upping the last of their lobster traps and preparing to row for home. They waved enthusiastically to him and shouted happy greetings.

Their cheer washed over him as if in a dream world and he pretended at a carefree response. But one glance down into the boat, where his feet braced against the oars, stripped his optimism. The hull was awash with water that had shipped aboard as the dinghy had punched out through the waves from the beach.

In that water, the carcass of the hated Bosun sloshed back and forth with each surging pull on the oars.

The man's gaping wound yawned as wide as a gutted sheep, the crimson water washing and re-washing the tattered meat, painting and re-painting the inside of the boat with dire accusation.

Chikunda felt transfixed by it.

He looked at the lifeless thing there and then across at the cheerful men singing overtures of heroism to him in their unique, toothless colourful manner. They recalled in poetic prose the quickly growing legend that his exploits in saving the shipwrecked damned had recently earned for him.

He wondered what they might think, if only they knew what cargo he carried.

Soon enough they would. Soon enough he would find out what they thought… if he lived that long.

"*Jy my broer,*" the closest of the boats yelled in the local dialect of Dutch, minus his front teeth. "*Jy't 'n fokken groot vis gevang, of 'n rob?* Or is that the Bosun asleep there?" the man asked, switching to English.

Then the man roared heartily.

Chikunda could not reply, fearing what he might say, but he knew well enough what the man had shouted, speculating if he'd caught a seal or was bringing in a large fish.

They'd seen it.

The man had guessed right and as he slid away from them, there was a vigorous debate between the seafarers speculating about it.

Rumour always ran through the town like wind over wheat.

Some, of course, would have seen the Bosun leading him up the mountain pass in the morning and everyone in town would by now have known where they'd been headed… to retrieve the boat.

Now that they'd spotted his load and made the connection, the stories would begin to fly and quickly embellish.

If he landed second to another boat on the beach, rumour would already be crackling through the town that the Bosun was mysteriously laying and not sitting in the boat.

He couldn't afford to lag.

He needed to land and get to the InDuna of the town—to the Governor—before the town criers got there first with an already elaborate account of what had *definitely* occurred.

He leaned on the oars with fresh vigour, pulling fast ahead of all others heading in the same direction.

And then he realized that he needed to get directly to the fort and as far from the gaggle and throng at the boat beach as possible.

Forgoing the safety of an easier and relatively wave-free landing at De Waterkant near the *Bree* or broad street, Chikunda aimed his bow directly for the fort.

This course took him on a close approach to the ships at anchor in the bay.

Up in the forest of masts, crew scampered about on the yards and rigging, working with the reefed sails of a frigate or making a ship of the line ready for departure. Their vantage allowed them to look down into his boat and no doubt observe the villainous, bloodied cargo it carried.

English shouts filtered down to him as he went by.

The beach in front of the fort was more exposed to the open ocean and picked up heavier swells, but it was a gamble he had to make.

Every few strokes, he looked over his shoulder and the surging bow to check his distance from the breaking surf line.

Up on the parapets of the fort, he could make out the Governor's wife at her easel. An artist, she would spend hours and days crafting one or another of the town's magnificent views into paint.

Today she had her back to the ocean with her easel before her, reproducing the magnificence of Table Mountain.

The closer he came, the more his worry grew.

A band of children had broken off from the traditional wave-free beach where boats landed and fish were sold.

They'd locked onto this more interesting prospect of a dinghy heading for the large dumpers at the foot of the fort.

They yelled and cavorted as they ran, signalling exuberantly to Chikunda to know why he was landing here.

It was a disaster.

The soldiers on the fort's parapets noticed and turned to watch.

Other stragglers, drunks and beachcombers joined in—some signalling urgently for Chikunda to head back to the safer beach, some calling their timing to help him come in between the wave sets.

He looked over to those from the fleet that he'd passed and saw that two of the boats were on the beach already, five cables of distance down the coast.

Now the panic started to rise.

He looked once more at the Bosun, dead and butchered in the blood-soaked boat, and in that death he saw his own body swinging from the gallows.

A set of waves passed, the last of the dumpers kicking spray so high that for an instant the fort and onlookers were gone, only the rock of Table Mountain's timeless outline remained, untouched by the hand of man beyond it.

This was the moment.

Chikunda leaned on the oars and began to build momentum to come in on the back of a smaller wave.

And then he saw it.

Out over the stern, toward the horizon, stood what looked like a reflection of the great mountain beyond the bow behind him.

It was colossal and already beginning to foam at its crest.

It was a freak set, the first in a train of waves that dwarfed all others that day.

It was too far to the beach to make it; Chikunda's only chance was to turn and face the curl.

He slammed his right hand forward on the oar, hauling with every sinew on the left oar—twice, three times, he pulled with the left, punched with the right.

The little boat rotated on its axis.

With the bow facing the onrushing wall of water, Chikunda stood on the oars, hauling till he saw bright bursts of colour before his eyes.

He dared not turn to look, it was terror enough to see the reactions over the stern of those on the beach screaming for him to make it, some laughing cruelly in anticipation that he wouldn't.

The air seemed to fizz with sound and then it detonated like the shot of a cannon and the whole dinghy shuddered.

It was over, the curl had beaten him.

Chikunda looked over his shoulder and in horror saw that the white water was as tall as a tree.

In that instant it hit him and the boat was gone from under him.

He was under, swirled round and round, explosions of white and dark behind tightly sealed eyes. Slammed into the sand below, spun and savaged by the fury of water, as if in the grip of a monster.

"Calm," he heard his mother's voice speaking Swahili in his head. "Be calm, my boy."

And Chikunda let himself go loose, let the water do with him what it will. "Thy will be done," he told himself in the savagery of the moment.

He felt another detonation of the next wave, and as his head broke the surface, there was just an instant to suck air and then the wave had him like a terrier with a rabbit.

"Calm!" the voice soothed him and he didn't fight. He let the wave tire itself out on his dead limp body, trying as it was to tear each limb off and twist it in a different direction.

A third detonation, the shockwave punching his lungs, then a little suck of air but mostly water and another brutal pummelling as the white water went over.

His lungs screamed for oxygen as slowly everything faded to black.

When he awoke, groggy and feeling near death, there was a forest of legs about him and a fire raged in his chest.

He tried to speak and it brought on a vomit reflex, a cup of saltwater belched through his lips, his lungs feeling ripped out.

Most of his clothes were torn away, but he didn't care. Another wave ran up the beach and the bystanders dragged him further onto dry land out of its icy grip as it washed around him.

"Was that the Bosun with you?" someone was asking him urgently. "Why was he lying down?"

"Has anyone seen him?" Others in the crowd picked up the call.

Chikunda was nodding weakly, still unable to speak.

"We saw him in the undertow. Was he ill?"

Chikunda nodded again.

"There's no sign of him," another voice spoke.

"Good!" someone called.

"I'll drink to that," another voice declared.

"Let's sit him up."

Strong hands grabbed Chikunda and brought him to a seated position. He felt drunk, beaten and hopeless.

"Lay him over the rowing seat," someone suggested. "I have seen that work."

They picked him up and dragged him.

His head hanging down, he watched his feet ploughing two furrows through the sand, and then the dinghy's gunwale went below his vision. They placed him on his knees inside the salvaged boat, the rowing seat pressing into his stomach.

"Get his head below the stomach, it lets the water out," the voice was instructing.

Strong hands once again did the bidding.

Through salt burned eyes, Chikunda focused at close range on the boat decking right where the Bosun had been lying, where all that water awash with blood had sloshed—and it was clean and pristine, the evidence washed away.

He tried to lift his head to see if it was true, if the whole boat had been cleaned by the pressure wash inside of the wave. The effort of trying brought on a convulsion and the last of the swallowed ocean came boiling out.

"There… it works, see!" the voice cheered triumphantly.

"Nobody seen that executioner pig?" The question was raised again.

"Naaagh, probably swept under. Let the fish have him if they dare. Best we stop looking lest we find the bastard!"

There was a chorus of laughter.

"And finish him with an oar if you do."

And then Chikunda heard a friendly, familiar voice beyond the throng around him.

"Where is this man?"

It was the doctor, the little man who looked so like a woman hurrying toward him.

"I saw the whole thing, James," the woman with him, the governor's wife, was saying. "From up there," she explained, pointing to the easel still standing on the parapet with its view of the mountain, "I could see down into the boat and that *awful* man was lying there looking sick as any dog. The whole town heard of his antics last night and it wouldn't surprise me if he was still drunk now. No doubt drowned, and good riddance, I say to that too."

Dog.…

Of all the words she'd spoken, dog was the one that rang through.

Where is Jack?!

And then he remembered that the dog had refused the ride.

"No doubt drowned, and good riddance I say to that too, James"—the words echoed in his head again. *They think the Bosun drowned…? Until he washes up hacked in half!*

But that was in the hands of fate, he decided.

It sounded so much like an alibi that Chikunda saw clearly how fate was intervening here, how those Apostles were not mere mountains, that the mountainous wave that washed the slate clean was no accident.

"Let God's will be done," he affirmed quietly again to himself.

"Do not fret because of those who are evil," the psalm played in his mind, "for like the grass they will soon wither, like green plants they will soon die away."

There was a commotion and suddenly the boat was a bevy of gangly legs and tongue and huge welcome.

Jack had uncannily navigated directly to the shore and was in the boat, furiously licking Chikunda with yelps of triumph. Someone grabbed him by the scruff of his neck and ejected him with a *yip* from the boat. Chikunda tried to protest but he was ignored.

And then the legs of the crowd parted and the doctor moved through the breach to him, the Governor's wife close at hand.

Beyond them, he glimpsed an angel.

A very pregnant angel.

Faith was hurrying towards him.

News travelled fast in a small town.

> THE END <

_____

Epilogue

Spring, 2017

Thank you for sharing this true story, embellished though it is for drama's sake.

The slave ship and its wreck really did occur in 1794 in a place called Clifton Bay, near Cape Town, South Africa.

Indeed, Captain Antonio Perreira was the Captain of this ship, the *São José de Afrika*. And the *São José* really did founder on the reef of Clifton 2nd Beach—where I was the second person ever to dive on her.

When a close friend discovered her lying in 6 metres of water. There was truly not much left, only beams wedged in the boulder field and conglomerate containing cannon-balls, parts of what we now know were shackles, copper sheathing for the hull and handmade nails.

Skoenmaker's Gat was the original name of Clifton, named after a runaway deserter, a sailor who became a cobbler and lived on Kloof Road under a huge granite boulder, right where the public thoroughfare, Clifton Steps, now exits from the lower Victoria Road.

Of the 400 slaves chained in the slaver's holds, 200 were salvaged and sold the next day in Cape Town.

Baai of von Kamptz became anglicized to the modern Camps Bay.

The mussel-shell strewn beach where Chikunda and Faith first hid does exist. It is today known as Maiden's Cover and Bachelor's Cove.

The story of Chikunda and Faith are fictions, but the other places and names are historical fact, and the situations sketched here are drawn from the historical record of Cape Town.

Gallows Hill is the site of the modern-day headquarters for Cape Town's traffic police.

The old stone fort still stands in the city, now a mile and more from the ocean, reclaimed and bristling with skyscrapers as it was.

The safe beach for landing was at Waterkant Street between Bree, Long and Loop Streets. That location is now a square, Thibault Square, full of pigeons, restaurants, tall buildings and pavement lifestyle.

Buitengracht Street echoes the name of the "outer channel" of the old town.

The Heerengracht is today's Adderley Street.

"One (drink) for the road," that we cheerily recite these days, is indeed derived from "one for the rope," as described herein.

Dreadful tortures were visited upon slaves at Salt River and Woodstock. These suburbs used to be a thriving beach community with a fine beach that ran out of the city. Today, you will know that beach location as a ten-lane highway on reclaimed land, with a concrete and steel jungle to the seaward of you where Duncan Dock, The Royal Cape Yacht Club and the military naval base (described in Praying Nun), *SAS Unitie,* now stands and vast ships moor in safety behind vast concrete wharves.

Down in the foundations of the city skyscrapers, lie the shipwrecks of almost four centuries of ships beached on this Cape of Storms during onshore winter northwester gales.

Were you to seek the spot where Chikunda's troubles finally ended in the surf and on the beach, you'd be standing on the rail tracks of the Cape Town rail station.

To affirm these claims, I offer you news of the shipwreck that caused this book and its prequel to be written.

Genesis of The Story

> Overview coverage
https://www.youtube.com/watch?v=HhJUE
OQzYDg

- **1794:** The *São José*, a slave ship owned by Antonio Perreira and captained by his brother, Manuel Joao Perreira, ran aground at Clifton, Cape Town carrying more than 400 slaves, *en route* Mozambique to Brazil.
- **1980s:** Treasure hunters—(indeed, a friend an myself… the author)—discovered the wreck of the *São José*, but mistakenly identified it as the wreck of an earlier Dutch vessel.
- **2015:** The Smithsonian Institute of Washington in collaboration with the Iziko Museum of Cape Town correctly identified the wreck.
- **2016:** I published "The Praying Nun"—my dramatized account of our discovery and a part-2, fictional account taking the reader aboard the fated ship.

- **2017:** The Reckoning is the story of one of the survivors.
- **2018:** The sequel to The Reckoning will follow that slave as he tries to survive the brutal 1790s into the 1800s.

Video Links About Slavery

- Story of Slaves Part 1
  https://www.youtube.com/watch?v=ak1SlHjFBbU
- Slaves Part 2
  https://www.youtube.com/watch?v=n26NRPtD-xw
- Slaves Part 3
  https://www.youtube.com/watch?v=nbyDcrGdtq8
- Slaves Part 4
  https://www.youtube.com/watch?v=Kpy7DqGTFt8

About the Author

Michael Smorenburg

Born in 1964, I grew up in a fabulously stable family with the best siblings one could ask for and an embracing community. I also landed with my *derrière* firmly in the proverbial butter in another way; home was a piece of paradise; the beach community of Clifton, Cape Town, South Africa.

Today, Clifton is world-renowned as a playground of the super-rich, but back then it was all a boy could want; a wild and bounteous Southern Ocean on the doorstep flanked by towering mountains on all sides, and precious few rules in between.

It was there that I fell in love with adventure and nature, which in turn prompted my endless questions about what made everything tick. Religion, back then, provided the stock standard answer, but as time went by, science increasingly won my inquisitive vote.

In my mid 20s, the travel bug bit, and when my head cleared, it was the millennium and I found myself living in San Diego, California, founding an online marketing company. Yet, Africa's gravity is strong, and I was drawn back home, where I have happily remained.

Humans are, of course, the universe finding out about itself. We are of nature; we are matter... the stuff of stars, all too briefly made conscious and self-aware. Each of us is privileged to add our small voice to the symphony of life.

This book and my other novels are my small contribution into that great chorus.

Wherever you may be in time and place, it's been a very great privilege to entertain and now chat with you.

Please do stay in touch:
- I use: #SlaveShipNOVELs
- facebook.com/MichaelSmorenburg
- www.MichaelSmorenburg.com/Reckoning
- MichaelStheWriter@gmail.com

Other Titles by Michael Smorenburg

A Trojan Affair *explores actual unfolding events.*

The silent heavens stretched above a pious town locked in the grip of drought have become valuable beyond measure—the fracking bounty below its feet... irresistible. When Dara, 17, half Indian and raised in Oxford, England, arrives in the heartland of a Calvinist bible belt—a place his astrophysicist mother has come to build the biggest infrastructure in the history of science, the $2.5-Billion SKA radio telescope—he becomes the lightening rod for the town's anger and suspicion of outsiders.
Based on actual unfolding events, A Trojan Affair is a contemporary geopolitical thriller where science, religion, politics, greed and racism collide, tearing a community apart and setting generations against one another.

LifeGames Corporation *is a psychological thriller with elements of horror & high-technology.*

Catherine's Ad-agency has won the most lucrative prize in the world—a *LifeGames Corporation* contract.
Everyone knows what LifeGames does: Immersive Virtual Reality training
And everyone knows that LifeGames certification is the ticket to the top of world politics, military and business. But the intricacies of LifeGames are a jealously guarded secret; a secret Catherine is at the threshold of learning... The first tantalizing fact; Artificial Intelligence runs the entire operation and hypnotizes candidates to believe that their simulation is reality.

To learn more she must cross a forbidden line. Indeed, to retain the contract, Ken, the narcissistic boss-man, has made it clear that crossing the line is a deal breaker.

Ragnarok *is a thriller with a plot like none you've ever imagined.*

Tegan Mulholland is a Hollywood Exec flying Paris to Los Angeles. A mid-air event off the coast of Newfoundland will change her life…
South of Australia, on the other side of the globe, a secret NASA Warp Drive test backfires—a column of spacetime warps in an unexpected way and two passenger planes ahead of Tegan's wink off the radar.
As the world deals with the seismic events and recriminations that follow, an instinct for connecting dots convinces Tegan that the sudden spate of brutal massacres along the Newfoundland coast is far more sinister than the Hells Angel turf war the authorities are claiming.
The key to the truth lies in the hands of Pete, the charming arms-dealer she sat next to on the fateful flight… the man Tegan has secretly fallen in love with.

The Praying Nun *is the prequel to this, THE RECKONING, novel*

A story in 2 parts, 'now' and 'then' — come along on a gripping saga of adventure, intrigue and discovery of a shipwreck that has no identity; until 30 years pass and the Smithsonian fills in the missing pieces — then leap back two centuries to witness a tale of disturbing brutality and exhilerating human courage… The Praying Nun will leave you shocked to the core and pondering human nature in all its forms.

Part I - A True Story of Discovery and Excavation, 1985
In 1985 an uncharted shipwreck was discovered off the coast of Cape Town, South Africa. Two divers, the author and his friend, salvage artefacts from the ocean floor and try to identify the ship's identity and cargo. In 2015 the mystery was finally solved by the Smithsonian Museum of Washington. The ship was the São José de Africa, a slaver that ran aground in 1794 with 400 slaves aboard, half lost on

that day, the other half salvaged and sold the next day to defray costs. At this time, the recovered artefacts reside in the National Museum of African American History and Culture in the US, in 2027 they will be returned to the Iziko museum in Cape Town.

Part II – A Love Story of Terror and Tragedy, 1794
Naked and shackled, Chikunda, and his new wife Mkiwa are heaved aboard the slaver São José off the coast of Mozambique, bound for the slave markets of Brazil. Once below decks, down in the stinking holds with 400 other captives, Chikunda instinctively knows that it will all be over. When the Captain discovers that Chikunda and his wife are Christians, the couple are spared a horrific fate below decks, but this reprieve does not protect them from what fate has in store.

The story of Chikunda and Mkiwa, though fictional, is based on the best-known facts about the ship and the slave trade in general as contained in records, news reports, and journals available at the maritime archives, through accounts reported by the Captain, crew and from others who witnessed the disaster and its aftermath.

LifeGames/Ragnarok sequel—*Coming Soon...*

The Manhattan Event—Worlds Collide *LifeGames*
Technology spreads its wings.

With Ken gone from the helm and the company's key technology mothballed, what becomes of LifeGames?

Of course—exciting things!

More than that, those who read my other novel, "*Ragnarok*—Worlds Collide", will be equally inquisitive as to the fate of "the missing planes".

Well… both of these matters are resolved in my new book to be published in early 2018.

Strangely, it is a novel that brings together the two plots (LifeGames & Ragnarok) into a single tale of deception, intrigue and mind control at the highest levels.

You're gonna love it!

Email me to get an early copy:
MichaelStheWriter@gmail.com